WRECKED

A DEVIL'S HANDMAIDENS MC NOVEL

ALASKA CHAPTER
BOOK 1

E.M. SHUE

Mountain
R♥SE
PRESS

Wrecked

DEVIL'S HANDMAIDENS MC
Alaska Chapter Book 1

AWARD WINNING AUTHOR
E.M. SHUE

Wrecked

DEVIL'S HANDMAIDENS MC
Alaska Chapter Book 1

Text Copyright ©2023 E.M. Shue

All rights reserved. This book or parts thereof may not be reproduced in any form, stored in any retrieval system, or transmitted in any form by any means—electronic, mechanical, photocopy, recording, or otherwise—without prior written permission of the publisher, except as provided by United States of America copyright law. For permission requests, write to the publisher, at "Attention: Permissions Coordinator," at the address below.

This is a work of fiction. Names, characters, places, and incidents either are the products of the author's imagination or are used fictitiously. Any resemblance to actual persons, living or dead, businesses, companies, events, or locales is entirely coincidental.

Cover Design and Formatting by Mountain Rose Press

Editing by Nadine Winningham of The Editing Maven

Cover and Interior Photos from DepositPhoto and AdobePhoto Stock

www.authoremshue.com

emshue.ak@gmail.com

❀ Created with Vellum

TRIGGER WARNING

Wrecked contains hot and steamy sex, profanity, drinking, off page physical abuse, teenage pregnancy, graphic violence, murder and may contain other content that could be sensitive to some readers. Wrecked is meant for mature reading audiences, 18+.

WRECKED

At seventeen Scout "Riddler" Keller was left wrecked. Destroyed by the boy she loved and left to pick up the pieces for a new life. She carries a piece of paper in her wallet with her every day to remind her to only trust the sisters in her club. They are her new family and have been there for her and her young daughter through the years.

Riddler was sure she'd never see Thad again. When she returns home after her father is brutally murdered, she doesn't expect Thad to be the investigator on the case. He wants to start over with Riddler, but she still has that paper as a reminder of what he did to her.

When several young girls disappear from the area and it ties into her father's murder, Riddler will call on her MC friends for help. But when the truth of who is behind it all is revealed, she'll have to protect herself and her family. Even if it means asking Thad to go against everything he has sworn to uphold.

Join Surprises from E.M. to be kept up to date.
https://bit.ly/SurprisesfromEM

For my Lathrop Homies

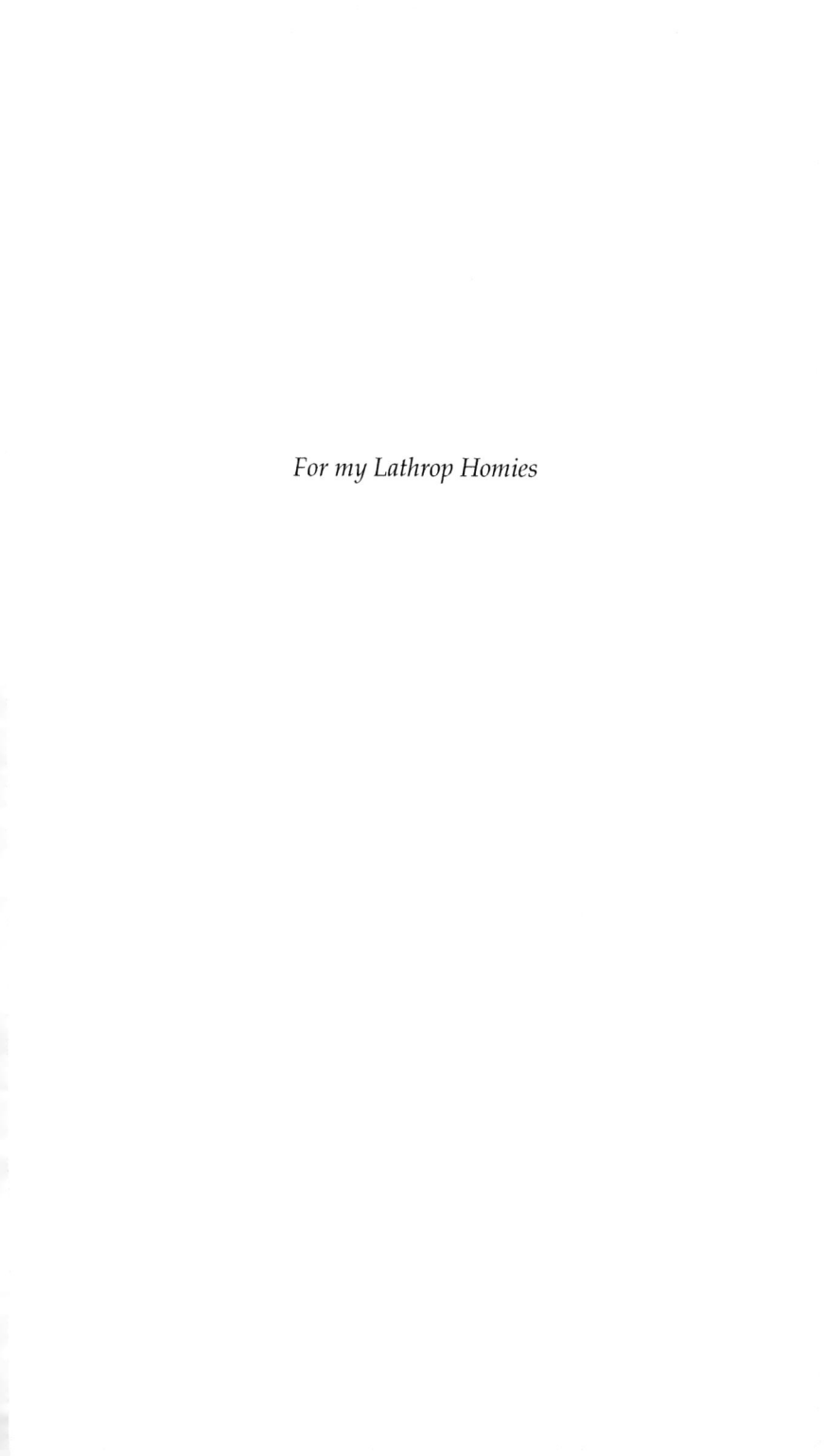

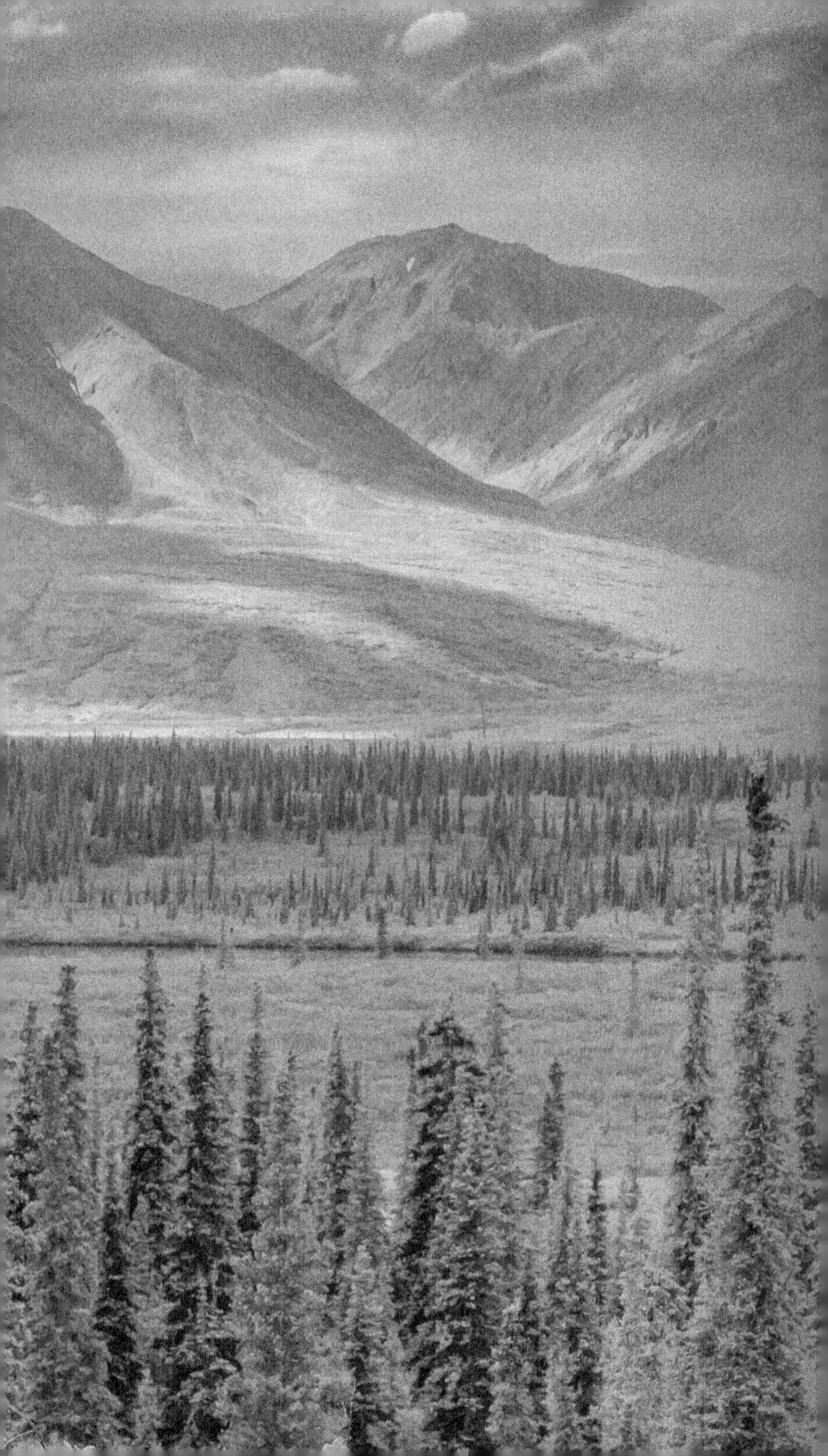

PROLOGUE

I'm moving along in the stolen pickup, my body bouncing from the bumpy road. The two-track trail that heads to a remote area I scoped out weeks ago is coming up. It's barely noticeable from the main road. The fact it's still bright outside is what allows me to work well after midnight. Land of the Midnight Sun, they call it. I call it annoying for sleep and a pain in the butt when I want to hide in the dark. I'm still getting used to all the daylight they have here, but I'll admit it's helpful for tasks like this.

I came here for a reason. To finally make her pay. But being able to move merchandise out of and through here has been a bonus for me. I've made more money in the short time I've been here than I ever did down south in one season. The bears will be on this one quickly, so there shouldn't be much evidence left over when all is said and done. It'll be chalked up to another runaway.

I make my turn and stop the truck when I reach the part of the trail I want. There is no place to pull over and park. I step out and take a look around. I'm on top of a large butte the locals call a dome because of its round shape. You can see for miles in almost every direction. The black spruce trees are sparse and spindly. This area of Alaska is mostly a soft tundra. In the distance I can make out a moose, the only witness to what I'm about to do.

Opening the bed of the truck, I glance around one last time before I grab the tarp and pull. The body hits the ground with a thud. I'm not concerned as she's already dead. I had to kill her when she kept screaming for help. Now, she'll be quiet as a mouse. It reminds me of the last time I broke a girl's jaw; she screamed and cried out too.

A sinister grin moves across my face at that thought. I bet I look like the Joker right now. I drag the tarp covered body over to the edge of the road. There is a steep embankment on this side. I unfurl the sheeting and hang on to it as I watch the body roll down the hill.

There's enough blood on the body that animals will smell it soon and come to inspect it. Aside from the bears and wolves, I bet smaller critters will find it too. Or even the large carrion birds.

"Lunch, boys." My voice carries in the quiet of the night.

I look down at my watch. I don't have much time to get back to Ptarmigan Falls to finish the next part of my plan. This means I'm going to have to rush and not enjoy myself with the next kill.

The perfect revenge can't be accomplished without the perfect bait, which I've got now. He's been sticking his nose into my business, and I can't have that. But more importantly, killing him will bring back the one person I need to finish all this.

A short twenty minutes later, I'm in the center of Ptarmigan Falls. The town sits near the Chatanika River and is a short drive from Fairbanks. It's geared for truck drivers. There's a gas station-convenience store, a café-style diner, and a few other small businesses, including the saloon, which is my destination.

I pull into the parking lot of the Keller Clubhouse Saloon. My hood is pulled low enough over my forehead so the exterior cameras on the premises won't be able to identify me. I've watched him for the last several nights. He closes at three in the morning. It takes him and the staff an additional half hour to an hour to clean up, then he sticks around to do the nightly drop in the safe. Tonight, being a Wednesday night, was a bit slower, and that's what I need. I move to the side door. It will be unlocked as he'll be coming out that exit soon. Folks around here think because it's a small, remote area no one would rob them or want to hurt them. Gullible idiots. I look back and notice the diner next door is still dark. This is the perfect time. No staff at either location means no witnesses to kill; however, the diner owner next door will meet her death soon enough.

My heavy boots thud as I slip through the door. I lighten my steps as I move toward the office where I know he'll be seated at the desk. I step into the light, and he pauses for a moment when he looks up. He must have heard me approach and assumed I was an employee who forgot something. Otherwise, he would be pulling one of the many guns I know he has hidden in the office. He's too trusting. He doesn't expect an enemy here. Little does he know he's not truly my enemy but a means to an end.

"Look, man, we open again later today at four. If you're here for money, I don't have much to give you. It's already been dropped into the locked safe and I can't open it for you." He points to the in-floor safe.

When he moves his chair back to stand, I pull my gun out and point it at him. I tip it slightly to indicate for him to stay where he is. I got the drop on him. He really wasn't expecting me. I'd be dead by now otherwise.

"I'm not here for money." I take aim. His face changes instantly. He holds up his hands like he can ward off what is about to happen to him.

"I have a family. You don't want to do this." His voice changes slightly as he begs.

I kind of want to hear him beg some more. In my moment of pause, he reaches under his desk. The old man tricked me. I can't forget he used to be in the military, he's trained.

I fire a shot. The bullet slams into his chest and he falls back in the chair, his body going limp. He coughs and I smile with joy. This is so much fun. I move across the room as I watch both of his hands to see if he'll go for the gun again.

"Don't you want to know why I'm killing you?" I ask, and he nods at me.

When I'm standing right in front of him, holding the gun to his forehead, I lean close. The blowback is going to get me, but I don't care. I plan on burning my clothes along with the truck as soon as I leave here. There will never be any trace of me, even the gun will be disposed of.

"I'm going to have so much fun fucking her up. Thank you for playing my game." I squeeze the trigger as his eyes flare wide at my words. The bullet cuts through his forehead between his eyebrows and exits out the back in a huge chunk with the chair. The wall behind him splatters in a fine pink mist of blood and brain matter. Blood sprays my face, and I can't stop the full-body laugh that breaks from my chest.

"I'm really going to enjoy this next part."

I notice his laptop and pick it up. I smash it into the wall until it's cracked and hanging by one hinge. I destroy his cell phone next, not sure if he could have somehow recorded this, but now I won't have to worry.

Stomping toward the exit because no one is here to hear me, I head back out to the truck to clean myself up and wait for the game to really start.

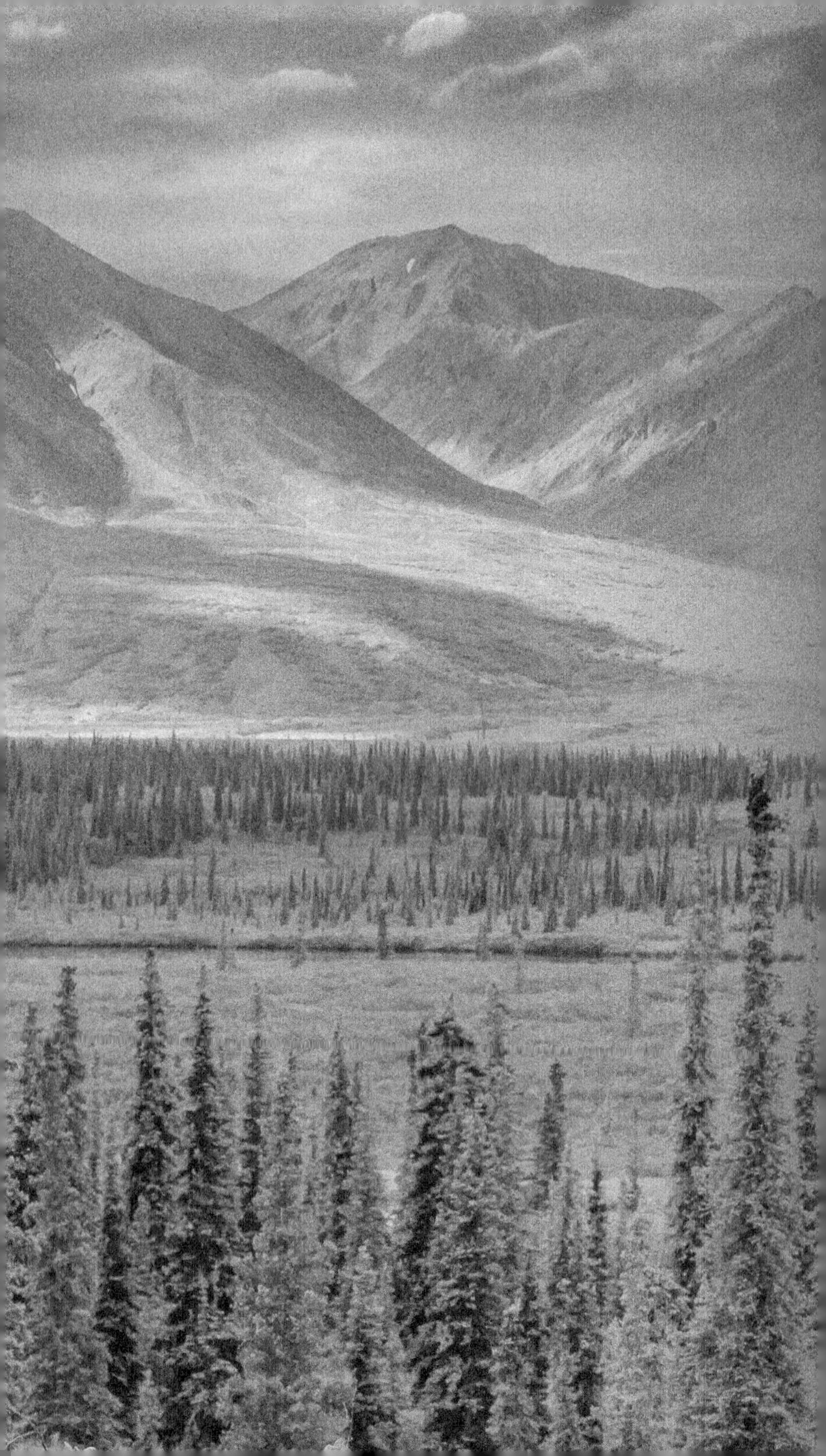

ONE
SCOUT

The three-hour drive from Tok Junction to North Pole has been easygoing. We stopped a couple of times so the girls could get off their rides and stretch their legs. It's not the length of time that was wearing on them but the fact the road is bumpy from frost heaves and none of them are used to driving on it. We had to get on the road early this morning because I'm anxious to get to my mom.

We pulled over at a rest stop for the night an hour after we crossed the border last night. My nerves are shot because this is the first time in ten years that I've returned home. My dad wanted me and Sky to come home so many times, but I couldn't do it. There are still too many memories and heartache associated with this place.

The last time I was here, I was a heartbroken teenager with a baby on the way. I made the choice to leave because I knew what the rumor mill would be spinning. Fairbanks and Ptarmigan Falls are both small towns, even though Fairbanks is the second largest town in Alaska. I ran before anyone could hurt me, and my best friend, River, helped. It's something she hated doing, but I begged her to do it. I played the best friend card hardcore. Something I still owe her to this day. I couldn't go on if my father looked down on me, and I knew he would. It's why I ran to Kentucky. I went to live with my aunt and had my daughter there. I've lived there for the last ten years, where I've built a life and a business.

My aunt is leading us through North Pole on our way into Fairbanks and then home to Ptarmigan Falls, which is about twenty-three miles north of the city. The plan was to always come home, but not this soon. I had a two to five-year plan in motion. But after the call I got two weeks ago, I couldn't leave my mother alone.

My mind replays that fateful call. *I was tuning up the motorcycle in front of me when the phone in my pocket rang. The beautiful beast sounded amazing, and the paint job I had put on it made it look like the beast it was. There was a dragon on the fuel tank blowing fire toward the ape hanger handlebars. I loved what Mercy came up with for the artwork. She'd been working with Jinx on designs. I planned on talking her into coming with me to Alaska when I was ready to sell and move out of state in a few years.*

I was so focused on my task of making the engine

sound and run like a dragon that I ignored the phone ringing in my pocket. I tweaked an adjustment and started it up again. Everyone knew if they wanted to talk to me, they needed to call the business line. The phone started up again, and this time I was frustrated. I shut off the engine, pulled the phone from my back pocket, and answered it.

"What?" I yelled into the phone as I ripped off my gloves and threw them on the bench, my anger getting the best of me.

"Scout, baby." I heard my mom's tear-filled voice. She and my father both flashed through my mind as I moved toward my office. Maybe something happened to Uncle Joel.

"What's a matter, Momma?" I had picked up some twang from living here so long.

"It's your daddy. He was found murdered this morning."

I dropped the phone as a pain-filled scream ripped from my throat. My eyes blurred and I couldn't see anything through the tears. Not my daddy. He was the man I measured all to. Most have been found lacking because he was so amazing. But he was everything. He visited me. He didn't make me feel guilty for the choices I made. He sent me money in the beginning to help until I got out of school and went to college. He was the one who gave my daughter her nickname, Little Bear. How was I going to tell her Papa wasn't going to be there for her? Everything I had done to stay away from Ptarmigan Falls rolled through my mind. I could have been there with him. If I had been there, would he have still been alive?

"Scout." *I heard my name yelled and reached for the phone as the door to my office shut.*

I looked up and saw River standing there. She had been with me for everything. She moved here shortly after I did, after losing her parents horrifically. She never questioned my decisions, just followed me. She was even my business partner. She reached for the phone and put it to her ear. I watched it all in a trance, not sure I'll ever be the same again.

"Hey, Momma Violet. Oh my God." Tears began to roll down her face. I cried too, the sobs racking my body now. "Okay. Let me get her under control and we'll call you right back." She hung up and dropped to the floor next to me where I rocked like a small child. She wrapped her arms around me. My daddy had been there for her too since losing his best friends in a head-on collision.

"My daddy is gone." I cried on her shoulder as she held me tighter.

"I know, Scout, but you have to pull yourself together. Your mom needs us."

I nodded and together we called her back.

"Momma, is that where Santa Claus lives?" Skyler's voice breaks me from my thoughts. Her soft Southern accent is laced with sleep from napping. This morning I woke her up early to get on the road. She's still in her unicorn jammies.

It took us almost two weeks to get ready and out of Widow's Creek. I left Mercy in charge of my shop down there. The president of the motorcycle club I'm in asked me to be the charter president here, another thing in the works that got moved up. A few of the girls came with me.

My aunt, Vixen, as she's called, is my charter treasurer. She was adamant about coming and said she needed to be with her sister. River, better known as Jinx, is my vice president. I couldn't think of anyone more qualified to help me. My best friend told me she couldn't let me go into the den of lions without her. I laughed at that one. It was the first laugh I had since I heard the news about my father. Minuet, or Frenchie, adopted me as her older sister and doesn't let me get far, so she came with us. Plus, she's been close to Skyler, and they are best friends. She wouldn't let Sky go far from her either. Frenchie is also our club secretary. When she decided to prospect to the club, I wasn't sure she could handle it after everything she went through. But she told me she had to do it to help other girls. I rescued her four years ago from a trafficker who was physically and sexually abusing her. She's been by my side since. Rounding out the crew who came with me are Keys, our hacker, and Ginger, my enforcer, who at this moment is in our tail gunner position, bringing up the rear and making sure no one sneaks up on us without letting me know.

"Yeah, baby girl." I chuckle as I look over at the almost fifty-foot-tall Santa Claus.

"Can we go?"

I look in the rearview mirror at her buckled into her booster seat. She hates the thing, but she still isn't quite tall enough for the adult seat belt to fit her correctly. I'm in my Super Duty F250 Crew Cab, pulling my fifth wheel toy hauler trailer. My business in Kentucky was thriving and I needed this setup to haul gear when we would go to races or car-motorcycle shows.

"Not today, we have to get to Grammy. She needs us." I reach up and finger my necklace as I think of my dad. The nut is from the first engine I worked on with my dad when I was a little girl. I stripped it, and he had it made into a necklace for me. The memories bring a burn to my eyes. I can't cry right now.

"Saturday." Skyler's voice again breaks me from my thoughts. I look over at Minuet, who is riding in the truck with us, she got tired of riding her bike.

"No, baby. How about the next Saturday?" I only look at her when I'm sure I don't have tears in my eyes. She smiles and holds up her hand with her pinky stuck out.

"Pinky promise."

I reach back and she hooks my pinky with hers. "Deal."

The smile I give her is completely forced because I can't show her how much pain I'm really in. I don't think it has fully hit her yet, but Saturday it will when we have the funeral.

"Did you hear that, Rufus? We are going to go see Santa Claus." Skyler hugs our big red and white Alaskan Malamute. He licks her face, and she laughs out loud.

I fight the urge to get off the highway and take the

long backroads to Ptarmigan Falls just so I can avoid Fairbanks. I'm shaken from that thought when I hear a Harley's loud pipes. I look in the side mirror and see a biker who isn't Ginger.

"Hey, Prez, we got a welcoming committee," Ginger says through the radio system.

As we pass through the last part of North Pole, more bikes move into position around my truck and trailer, leading us home. It causes a lump to form in my throat and my eyes to tear up again.

My father's saloon catered to all local bikers, those patched and those not. He welcomed everyone. This is a show of their respect for him. That first biker must have been a lookout and has called more.

By the time we pull up to the Airport Road light in Fairbanks, I'm surrounded by at least twenty bikers. They aren't all patched, but they are here and that's what counts. I look down Airport Road to the left into the core of Fairbanks and my heart aches from the memories of my youth. Looking to the right, I see the army base and know Jinx probably has lots of memories of there. That was where her father was stationed before he died.

The light turns green, and I slowly pull forward until we are fully rolling again. Part of me wishes I was on my bike too, but I need to be right here. Besides, I wouldn't be able to ride with all these guys right now.

By the time we reach the edge of Fairbanks and head toward Hagelberger Hill, another fifteen bikes have joined us. The sound of all the pipes causes my body to tremble. I've always loved the sound of engines, and motorcycles were my thrill before I was even allowed to ride. It took everything in my dad to keep me from his motorcycle and his classic pickup. I look out my windshield and take in the view stretched out before me. The last time I saw it was the day I decided to leave Ptarmigan Falls. The day I decided to run.

"Little Bear, get ready," Jinx says from the radio, and I look back to see my daughter. My reason for every choice I've made is looking excitedly in front of us. As we crest the hill, you can look over the valley where Fox is and, in the distance, you can make out the ridge where the Elliott Highway heads toward home. "Here comes the pipeline on your right." Jinx directs Skyler, who squeals in delight.

"Papa showed me pictures of that," she yells, and I can't help the real smile that tips up my lips this time.

We continue through the small town of Fox, where the weigh station for trucks is, and then continue on the Elliott Highway for another twelve miles. Finally, we enter the town my grandparents started back in the fifties. It really boomed in the seventies when the Trans-Alaskan Pipeline was being built. I turn into the driveway of the Keller Clubhouse and Saloon. I pause for a moment before getting out. I lean forward and rest my head against the steering wheel as the emotions wash over me. I feel a hand on my shoulder.

"It's okay, Momma. I got your back," Skyler says as I hear her belt click. She stands up and also places her hand on my shoulder. I swallow several times to ease the pain until a soft knock sounds on my window. I make sure I'm not crying when I look out and see my uncle standing there. He reminds me so much of my daddy and I can't stop the tears. The door opens and he pulls me into his arms.

"I got you, girl," he says against my hair, and I hold on tight.

I need to address all the bikers who have come to show their support. I pull back and take several big breaths before I reach into my truck to pull out my leather jacket with my cut on it. I got my President rocker added right before I left. The day Brazen slid it on me is a day I'll never forget. She was so proud of me. I was worried and sick to my stomach from all of the responsibilities I would have. She leaned in and gave me a good piece of advice.

"Don't ever let them know you can't handle it," she whispered in my ear as if she knew what I was thinking.

I stand here now and look at everyone.

"I really appreciate all your support and the wonderful escort today. I'll see you Saturday."

I look at the road where a trooper vehicle is parked because they can't get into the parking lot with all the motorcycles. I turn to see Minuet behind me with Skyler in front of her.

"Frenchie, take Little Bear inside and don't come

out until Jinx or I come get you." She doesn't question me, she does as she's told. Rufus follows along, always protecting Skyler.

I watch as the trooper exits his vehicle. I can't believe it's him. He has a swagger now that he didn't before. His body is bigger than I remember it being. He's even taller than I remember. The Alaska State Trooper uniform molds to his chest, the slacks strain around his large thighs. My heart thumps harder in my chest. I feel my nipples grazing against the lace of my bra. Fucking traitorous body.

He stands back at the edge of the driveway as motorcycle after motorcycle pulls away, heading back toward town. I'm going to have to open soon for them. My father's patrons are loyal and will be missing this place before long. Even in the winter when they can't ride their bikes, locals would drive the distance to come sit and visit with others.

"I thought you were going to be later." My mother wraps me in her arms. I wish I had gotten either of my parents' height, but I came in at barely five foot five while my mom stands at a statuesque five foot ten. My father was six foot three. I wear heels to make myself look taller when I'm not working.

When all the cycles are out and the only ones remaining are ours, he moves toward me. The hat sits low over his eyes so I can't see them, but I remember what they look like. The beautiful blue always reminded me of the sky on a cold winter day. My heart clenches at that thought. I can't and won't go there right now.

When we crossed the border into Alaska, one of the things we did first was get out our guns and start carrying them again. We respected the laws of Canada and kept them locked up, but now I'm currently carrying in my holster at my low back, as well as most of the girls. Here in Alaska, we only have to identify to the police that we are concealing and carrying. I wouldn't be surprised if Ginger has a couple under her leather jacket.

I feel the girls come in behind my mother and me, supporting us both. When he's finally standing in front of me, I feel his eyes moving over my body. I try to hold in the tremble as much as possible. I don't want him to see I still have a reaction to him. That after all these years, I still feel something. I shouldn't, but I do. He nearly broke me, and I can't let him see I still care. Besides, I still have the proof of how much he *cared* for me. I carry it with me every single day to remind me to never trust a man again.

Thad

I look her up and down from the tip of her toes to the top of her blond head. I don't miss the motorcycle cut with the President patch on it. I saw one of the girl's backs. Devil's Handmaidens is a new club to the state. I'll have to do some research when I get back to the station. I look over and see her mother and uncle along with a blonde I've never met. The woman looks so much like her mother, it must be the aunt she used to talk about. A movement on the other side of Scout catches my attention and I see River. The hate coming from River's eyes almost causes me to step back. I don't understand it. She and I always got along, we never had any problems.

I turn back to Scout and swallow before I say her name. I've only spoken her name a few times since I last saw her ten years ago. She was the sweet, beautiful sixteen-year-old girl who stole my heart. I was a lovesick eighteen-year-old who let her stomp all over said heart. It took me years before I trusted women again. Then I married a complete bitch. The only thing good that came from that marriage was my son.

"Scout." I'm proud my voice didn't crack. The woman who broke me shivers ever so slightly and pushes her sunglasses to the top of her head. I look down into her pale hazel eyes and see the slight reddening from her crying. She has small freckles across her nose and cheeks. The urge to kiss them all almost overwhelms me. Why does she still have this control over me?

Her skintight leather pants and tank top pulled down enough that I can make out the swells of her full breasts show off her extra curves. I notice the necklace around her neck sitting against those plump breasts and I fight the urge to ask her to cover herself.

"Thaddeus," she says my full name but not breathlessly like she used to. Instead, it sounds stilted and formal. I look at her again and notice how tight she's holding herself. I can make out her pulse thumping in her neck. She's nervous and upset about something. It has to be about her father, not me. She's the one who broke my heart.

"I was dropping by to speak to your mom, but since you're here I have some questions for you too."

"Shoot." She acts like there was never anything between us. As if we parted as friends and not lovers.

"Where were you two weeks ago? Do you have any enemies?" I scoff. "I mean, do you have any enemies that would come after your family?" I know I'm stereotyping her because of the MC affiliation, but after the show I just saw with both clubs, coalitions, and two-percenters, I have to wonder.

I hear the restlessness of the shuffling boots from her club members at my insinuations. An extremely tall redhead is watching me close. I could tell the moment I walked up that most of them were carrying guns.

"Now, Trooper Abbott, if you have an issue with my niece, I have to tell you—" Joel starts, but Scout holds up her hand, stopping him.

My girl has changed. She's no longer timid and shy. She doesn't let others answer for her. She moves a bit closer to me and tips her head to the side. The scent of citrus and spice that has always been her carries to me instantly. It's a smell that causes my cock to react to this day. I hate my body for this betrayal.

"Trooper Abbott." She sneers at my name, and I want to shake her or kiss the fuck out of those lips. "I was in Widow's Creek, Kentucky, until four days ago when I started driving here." Her soft voice has a commanding tone to it that I've never heard from her before. She chuckles softly and it's not in humor. "As for enemies... Well, anyone who goes against me is an enemy." She pauses and looks me square in the eyes. "Anyone who hurts me is my enemy." The biting tone of her voice doesn't make her look any less sexy.

My chest aches and my breathing increases. I'm about to step into her personal space when her mother saves us both from something embarrassing. The thought of fucking her against the side of her lifted truck is almost overwhelming. I can't think with my little brain trying to take over.

"Thad, you didn't mean anything bad now, did you?" her mother says. "You just need to rule out everyone. I already gave you my alibi, and you just heard Scout's. Want River's next?" I step back and so does Scout. I look over at River, who is looking between Scout and me.

"Answer him, Jinx," Scout says, and again I hear the authority in her voice that wasn't there before.

The girl I fell in love with was soft and quiet unless it had something to do with engines and cars. This woman in front of me is commanding, and I can tell in the way she shifts she has some combative training. It makes me wonder why she would do that. Why she would want to be trained.

"I was with Riddler. She and I lived together. I believe at the exact moment, I was in the paint booth of our shop spraying down a Barracuda. Keys?" she says, and I don't understand what she means until a brunette a couple of inches taller than Scout steps forward.

"I didn't know the victim, but I've known Riddler since she and Jinx were both prospects. As for the date and time, I was working in my room at the DHMC clubhouse. I can provide computer documentation as proof of timestamps. Ginger?"

The tall redhead steps up next and looks me up and down before she shakes her head.

"I was asleep. Maybe I did it," she scoffs.

"Ginger." The tone coming from Scout stops her.

"I wasn't in Alaska until last night for the first time." I can hear the sarcasm in her tone, and I turn back to Scout.

"Riddler?" It suits her. Scout used to love riddles and puzzles. That's what an engine was to her, a puzzle she needed to complete. Make it run better and sound louder.

The blonde I clocked earlier steps forward. "I'm Vixen. I was busy at home." She doesn't say anything else to clarify, but a hush works over the group. I turn back to Scout again, and she shuffles on her heels slightly. Something is up with this statement, and I want to solve it. A need inside me to find out the truth pounds through my veins.

"Do you need to question all of us?" she asks softly, and for the first time I hear a tremble in her voice. Something scares her.

"I'd like to."

"Jinx, go relieve Frenchie and send her out. You know what to do."

River moves from the group to the saloon entrance. After she steps inside, another blonde steps out, this one is shorter than Scout. She's extremely petite and walks over to us.

"Prez?" Her voice has a slight accent to it.

"Frenchie, this officer would like to know where you were on May tenth at about four in the morning Alaska time, that would be eight Kentucky time."

She looks at Scout and then toward me. "Officer, I was in school." I hear the French accent now.

"There, you've heard our alibis. Now why don't you go do your job and find out who killed my father." She stutters over the last part, and again I feel myself wanting to pull her into my body and comfort her. I know she's hurting. I've been because Levi was a good friend to me. He always told me he regretted that Scout and I didn't work out.

"I was returning these also. I'd like to look around the office if I could?" I hold out a bag containing her father's watch and rings. They all look back at the building and then to me.

"No," Scout and her aunt say at the same time as her mother says I can. I look between them and take Violet's suggestion over Scout's. When I start to move around them to head that way, Scout steps in front of me.

"I said no." Her voice quivers ever so slightly again, and I watch as she pulls back a foot into a fighting stance.

"You don't want to do this, Sunshine." I lean down toward her as I pull my hat off. I watch her breath hitch at the nickname I used to call her. I'll take her down if I have to in front of her people. "Are you interfering in my investigation? Or threatening me?"

"Now, now. Trooper Abbott, you don't need to search the office again. It's been cleaned already. Besides, Ms. Keller just got home after a long, stressful drive. I'm sure she'll rethink this, say Monday?" Joel tries to move between us, but I hold my hat up in his face, stopping him. I don't take my eyes off her though.

"What's it going to be, Scout?" Calling her Sunshine was just a slip of the tongue.

She pulls her bottom lip between her white teeth before letting it go, and her sweet little tongue tips out to lick it. My palm itches to take her waist and pull her close. My body is begging me to kiss her.

"Monday," she says, and I step back. I can't force the issue without a warrant. I hand her the bag with her father's belongings and turn back toward my vehicle to get away before I risk my career.

When I make it back to my SUV, I see that she is still standing there watching me. I pull away and make a U-turn to head back toward town and my life that doesn't include her. I watch her in my rearview mirror as she moves toward the entrance of the bar.

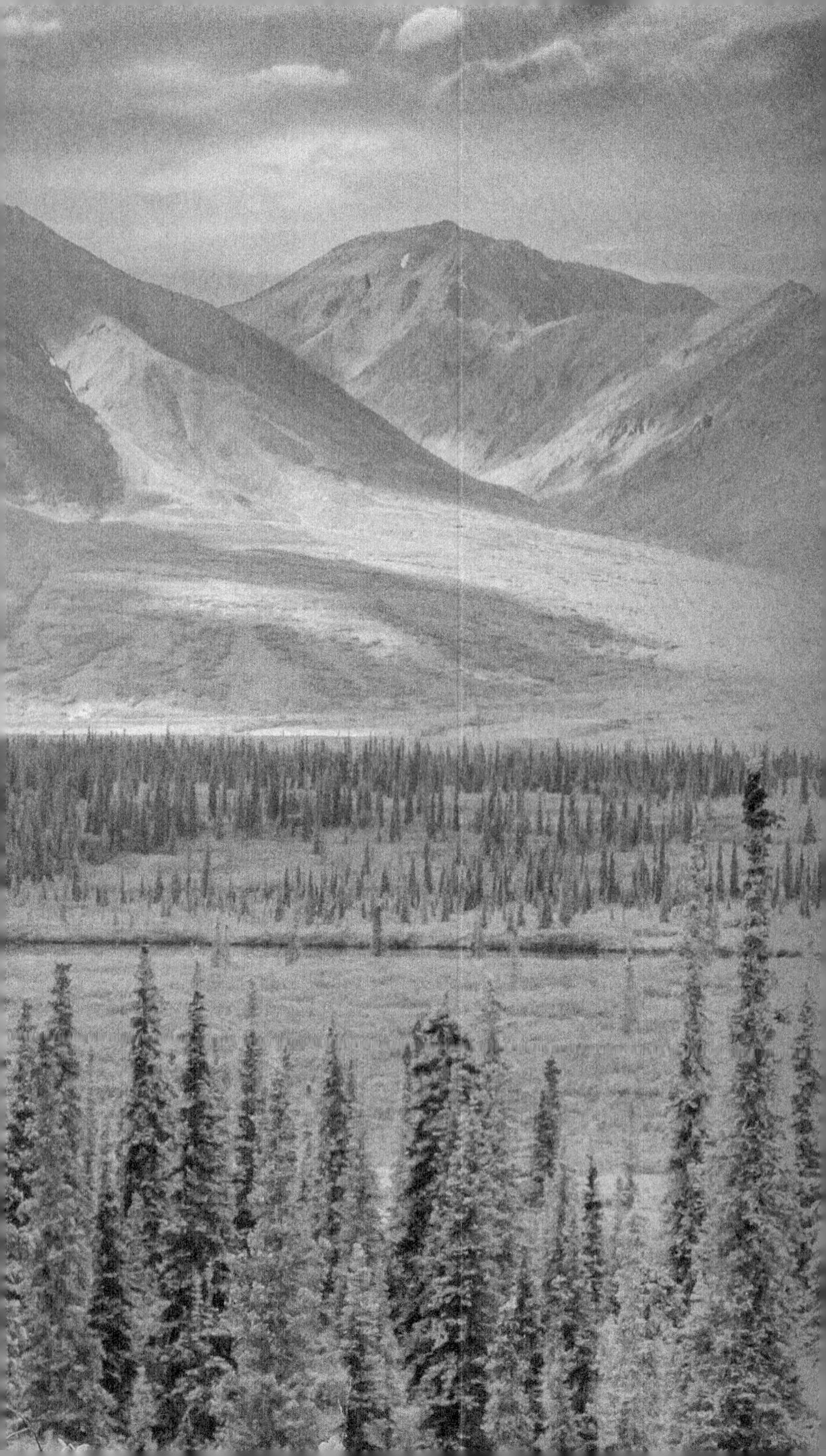

TWO
SCOUT

As I sit in the back of the limousine holding Skyler's hand, I try to hold in the tears. Yesterday we unloaded as much as we could from my trailer and helped my mom get ready for today. The places my father set up for us before he died are amazing. He had the original roadhouse turned into a clubhouse for the Handmaidens. There are plenty of rooms for everyone to stay in.

Mom wanted Sky and me to stay with her until they finish my apartment next week. Even though we'd planned to move here in a couple of years, it was as if my father knew something would get us here sooner. He had the original automotive repair garage that my grandfather opened completely redone. The upstairs is an apartment where Sky and I will live.

The rumble of all the pipes from the motorcycle

escort doesn't even comfort me. For once the sounds cause my body to tense. My father didn't want a church service. He always wanted a graveside service and a wake at the saloon.

As the limo turns toward the Birch Hill Cemetery, my gut clenches. This is it. My father will be laid to rest next to his parents in the cemetery on the hill overlooking Fairbanks. I'll never be able to hug him again. I won't hear him tell me that I made the wrong choice. He only found out about my secret a couple of weeks before he died. It hurts that our last conversation was a fight. He was so mad at me.

I pull my bottom lip between my teeth and bite down. The pain is becoming too much. I feel a hand on mine and look back over at my mom.

"It's okay, baby girl," she reassures me. But she doesn't even know yet. I need to tell her.

As the limo pulls up, I see all the cars lining the area. There are so many people here to celebrate my father's life. But it's the tall man in the black slacks and black button-down shirt that I can't take my eyes off. His body is rocking and calling to me in a way I don't want it to. Standing next to him is a little boy who is an exact miniature of him.

His sister is standing with him also. She showed up yesterday to help. Her deep purple hair is up in a bun and she's in a black dress. She'd been working for my father as a bartender for a while now. I couldn't hide my secret from her, but she hasn't confronted me yet. Part of me hopes it will never come out, but I know it's just a matter of time.

The door to the limo is opened and everyone else gets out. I sit with Sky and my mom for a moment longer, not ready for this. When my uncle reaches back in, he takes my hand and I step out on my shaky legs. My high heels sink into the gravel, and I steady myself. I reach in and help Skyler out and hold her hand tight in mine. Joel helps my mom next and doesn't let her hand go as we move to the back of the hearse where my father's casket is waiting.

Several of my father's friends surround it, and I watch as they lift it up and carry it to the stand it will sit on during the ceremony. We follow behind and I can't stop the tears now. They flow down my face and choke me. I can barely see through them. Skyler leans into me more and I reach down to pick her up in my arms. Even at almost ten, she's light enough I can still carry her. She buries her face in my neck and I feel her tears against my skin.

As the funeral goes on and on, I can feel his eyes on me as I hold Skyler on my lap and then move her to the seat next to me. She never releases my hand. Anyone outside my circle would know she's my daughter, just like I know the little boy with him is his. We both moved on with our lives.

Thad

. . .

I can't take my eyes off her or the little girl. Both are dressed in black dresses. The girl, Skyler—according to my sister is her name—has hair the same color as her mother's, but her eyes are a blue from this distance. She looked over to me once, but she won't let go of her mother. This has to be the child she had when she cheated on me.

The rumor mill had said she had an abortion and that's why she left Fairbanks. But this child is around the right age. I still can't believe that as soon as I left, she turned to someone else, but here is the proof.

When Scout finally looks over at me, I see the devastation in her eyes. She's been crying silent tears since she walked up. This has to be hard for her. I know from talking to her father before he died that they weren't as close as they used to be, but he still used to travel down to see her. He never once mentioned he had a granddaughter. Levi also didn't talk about Scout much with me after I told him I didn't want to listen.

Scout's hair is down, hanging around her shoulders, and the sun is reflecting off the blond strands. She's in a form-fitting black dress with long sleeves. I can see the ink along her arms and hand. I don't know how I missed those on Thursday when I was questioning her, but I notice them now along with all the gauges and piercings in her ears. She even has a small diamond in her nose that I missed too. I was so focused on seeing her, I didn't really see her.

She, again, is surrounded by members of her club and probably every other biker in Fairbanks and those that drove up from Anchorage and other communities. Her father was well known in the biker community. He never had any affiliations, and he welcomed all. It's one of the angles I've been investigating. Did someone in the community have a grudge against him? That is the reason I questioned Scout.

When the funeral ends, I watch as the family stands and everyone walks over to the casket and puts a flower on it. Scout moves over and unwraps a band from her wrist, then drops it with a flower onto his casket as it's lowered into the ground. I can make out that it's black leather and braided. I'm still watching her as she moves away from the crowd and stands off to the side. Her daughter remains with the petite blonde, Frenchie.

"I'll be back," I say to Stormy, who nods and takes Ryder's hand in hers.

I move toward where Scout is standing. A man walks up and offers his condolences. When he touches her arm, I want to rip it from his body for touching her, but I keep still.

"Thad," she says my name softly as she pulls her sunglasses down over her eyes. I move toward her and pull her into my body. It's the first time I've touched her in ten years. Her body is stiff, but she relaxes as I pull her into me tighter. Just holding her for this moment is like coming home. Every woman who came after her was compared to her. I thought I was going to have forever with her.

"I'm sorry for your loss, Scout. He loved you dearly and talked about you every chance he could. Told me how proud he was of you for opening your own shop and running it." The words flow as I lean down and inhale her spicy scent. It's all her. I've never smelled the combination but on her, and I do everything I can not to get hard.

She steps back and looks up at me. I see the tears rolling from under her glasses, and I reach out, dragging my hand along her cheek, to wipe the tears away. The distance between us now is as great as the Grand Canyon. She puts those walls up and reinforces them.

"Thad, I can't do this." She chokes on the words and steps back further from me. "I'm too vulnerable, and it isn't right. We are done and I'm never going back there again." Her words don't have any force behind them. They are soft and full of hurt. A pain that isn't just the loss of her father. Something else is hurting her, and I want to know if it's the same pain I feel.

"We were once friends." I remind her, and she pulls her glasses up to look at me. I want to be closer with her, but I also want to see if we can have more.

"I—"

"Mommy." The musical Southern accented voice comes from the little girl. She starts to move toward us, but River stops her, and I wonder why. They turn and move back toward the limo. Before I can say anything else, Scout is around me and moving away.

"I'll see you Monday," I say in parting, and she holds up a hand to me in response.

A couple of hours later, I'm standing looking down at the water of the slough not far from Goldstream Creek. Many nights after practice I'd meet Scout here and we would make out. The first time I brought her here was after the homecoming football game. We didn't go to the dance like she'd told her parents. We'd just started dating. I had broken up with my long-time girlfriend over the summer, and when school started, I instantly fell for the only girl in the automotive class I was taking at the University of Fairbanks. Like me, she was too advanced for the classes offered at Lathrop, so she went up there. I was in the class to help me get a jump start in moving toward a career in the military as a helicopter pilot. I knew if I had some mechanical experience it would help. I didn't know I'd enjoy turning wrenches, but as soon as I saw shy Scout in the class I was sold.

She had a love for every engine but especially

motorcycles and classics. She'd been up there for a year already, and I asked if she could tutor me. At first, she declined, and I chased after her. I bugged her in the halls at Lathrop and then in classes on campus. She wasn't quite sixteen and her mother had to drive her to and from campus. It took me one time and her mom agreed to let me drive her.

My Sunshine was pissed and wouldn't talk to me. She was such a tomboy back then. I remember my ex, Monica, and her crew of cheerleader friends would try to harass Scout, but River would stand up with her and they'd leave her be.

I finally had to tell Monica it was never happening again. My mom, even to this day, wishes I'd get together with her, but I won't. I found out she spread rumors after I left for the military that we were engaged, and I was pissed. I sometimes wonder if that's what made Scout cheat on me, but nothing makes cheating acceptable.

I bend down and pick up a rock to throw in the water. I watch the ripples as they flow away. That's what her cheating did, it caused a ripple in my life. I did become a helicopter pilot. But I also married a woman I knew I was going to divorce the moment I said, "I do." It still pisses me off, but I have Ryder and that's all that counts. I love my son.

I need to put Scout and her life behind me. This is the closure I was looking for. I'll investigate Levi's murder because I owe him that, but I don't care about Scout. I can't. I have to focus on my life.

As I pull away from the access, I see a motorcycle coming from Goldstream Road toward me. I watch in my rearview mirror as it pulls off where I just was. Part of me wonders if it's Scout and she's going through the same memories I was.

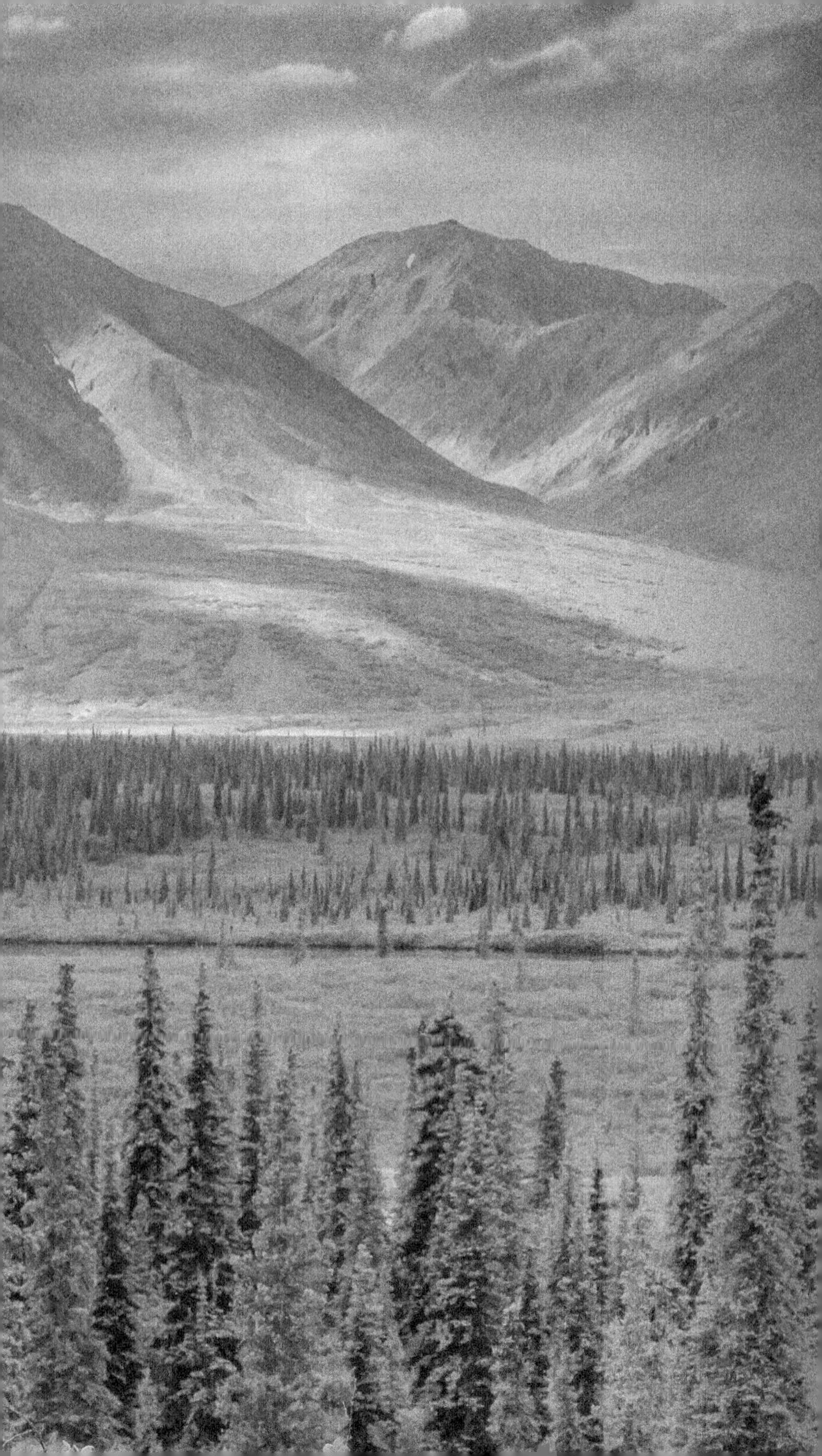

THREE
SCOUT

I move out of the bay toward the office at the back of the shop. I pass several stalls that have cars or trucks needing work. I need some help. Jinx is in her own area of the shop in a full paint booth with prep and mixing areas. My father made sure we had everything we'd need to start up our business here. I only had to finalize the installation of the separate ventilation systems.

In the two weeks that I've been back in Alaska, I've been crazy busy with settling my father's estate, getting the girls settled, and several new girls showing up. Then people started dropping cars and motorcycles off at the shop even before I announced I was opening it.

I sit down at the desk and dial up an old friend I know who might want to help me. She's currently a nomad with DHMC, but I bet she'd come help me out. We have a run tomorrow, and if she was here, it would help us out a lot.

"Riddler, what can I do for you?" A husky voice comes across the line.

"Rivet, how would you like to come to Alaska? I could use a good wrench turner and maybe a sergeant." I've already talked to Jinx and the other girls about this. They also want me to contact another nomad we know. I'm still waiting on that one because she has never wanted to settle down.

"You run into issues?" I like that she gets right to the point, no small talk.

"Nothing major. The troopers still haven't figured out who killed my father. The locals think it was a stranger who thought he had money, but he'd already done the nightly drop." I don't tell her that I have some suspicions. That I've been getting some weird emails.

"I'll be there in two weeks. I'm in Seattle now and between jobs. I'm helping a friend here, then I'll be there."

"Thanks, girl." I hang up and look at the clock on my computer.

"Jinx, time to call it quits," I announce through the intercom system, knowing she'll hear me because she doesn't have music playing right now. "I'm going to go shower."

I move through the building to the door that leads up to my apartment. I unlock it with my fingerprint and head up, knowing that Sky is with Frenchie and

Mom in town doing some running around. I still need to sit my mom down and talk to her, but she's been busy trying to get the café going again after she took off some time.

I let the water slide down my body, wetting my hair down completely. Memories of Thad have been coming in the form of nightmares lately. I remember every moment he and I had.

The worst of them was last night. I woke up with my clit throbbing. My naked body writhing around on the bed. I need a release so badly, but I'm not ready to find someone local. Something in my gut keeps me from doing it.

It's been at least two to three long years since I've had a lover. Shit! This isn't cool that I finally have the need for someone, and I can't because I'm worried he'll find out. Who the fuck cares when he's the one who fucked me over.

I sit down on the ledge in the huge shower my dad had installed. I don't know why he thought I'd need a five-bedroom apartment above the garage. Sky and I only needed a two-bedroom. River is staying here too, but she also has a room in the clubhouse. Same with Minuet. We all have rooms in the large clubhouse. And my aunt is currently staying with my mom.

As I sit on the bench, I think about trying to get myself off to take the edge off, but I can't do that either. I stand and rinse instead, needing to get ready.

This is the first Friday the saloon will be open

since my dad's death. We had the wake there, but I didn't stay. I had to go for a ride, and I found myself in the one place I shouldn't have gone.

Our place.

The place where Thad first kissed me. The place we made out at. Where we did it in our cars after our first time when he took my virginity at the hotel where his prom was held. So many memories I have of that small pull-off on Ballaine Road. As I was driving up, I noticed a large Dodge pickup pulling out. I'm glad they left before I got there, I didn't need anyone observing my breakdown. I cried for my dad and for the loss of Thad too. What could have been if Thad didn't break my heart.

After I dry off, I step into my large closet and start grabbing clothes. I'm not riding, so I can wear heels and lighter leather. I'm glad I have my cut in the heavy leather and a second in the softer leather for nights like this. I slip the black thong up my legs and then my skintight leather pants with lace cutouts. The red bustier is next. I don't need a bra since my top has built-in cups and cinches tightly, keeping my full B cup breasts in place. I was a small A cup before I had Sky. I lean over to pull the girls up so they show a perfect amount of cleavage. Standing in front of my full-length mirror, I take myself in. I need to finish my hair and makeup, but I'm looking pretty fuckable in the red and black look. I love that the bustier has an overlay of black lace and black ribbons and allows just the right amount of skin to show.

Okay, so I'm going to see if I can get a good wall fuck tonight out of this outfit. I don't care if he finds out. He made his choices a long time ago.

I step back into the bathroom. Since moving here, I met a new hairdresser and changed my look. I cut off all my long hair for a short, funky style. Because my face is wider at the cheeks and forehead, I have to be careful how I style my hair so it doesn't look fuller. My new hairdresser talked me into a shaggy bob. I also have long sideswept bangs. I style it the way she showed me, completely in love with the style. It fits my cut from the past. Stepping forward into my future without all the baggage of my youth. I darken my eyes with thick liner and give myself the perfect cupid's bow red lips.

"Hey, Riddler, you in here?" I hear River's voice and look at her in the mirror. "Damn, girl, you trying to get fucked tonight?" She moves next to me, and I take in her outfit.

"Look who's talking." I wave my hand at her outfit. She's dressed like me but in all black. Because she's taller than me by several inches, her heels bring her height up to over six feet. Her facial piercings sparkle in the light. "Going to forget your past too?" She and I have no secrets from each other.

"No comment. But damn, girl, I love the red." She moves out to the bedroom. "You should see this." I join her and look out my bedroom window to the parking lot below us. The saloon just opened, and it's already packed with a line.

"Shit, we are going to be busy tonight."

"No, you hired Stormy as your manager for a reason. She can handle this. You are going to go to the office and then out to listen to the music. Got it?" She points at me.

It's true. I hired Stormy, Thad's sister, as my manager because the other one didn't want to continue after my father's murder. Stormy is perfect. She's hired several new girls that will fit our new aesthetic of borderline biker bar-girls' night out club. Keys set up new security cameras and a better system of checking and verifying IDs. Ginger worked with the bouncers, teaching them better techniques.

The last two weeks have been busy. I can't believe we've gotten this much accomplished in such a short time.

I grab my boots and move out of the room, my nerves already climbing. I need a shot and some food. In my large kitchen with industrial appliances, I grab a sandwich my mom dropped off for me earlier when she picked up Sky. I take a big bite of it as I hear the clink of glasses. River knew what I needed.

River and I have been best friends since elementary school. Not many friends make it that long, but she and I have. We've never doubted that we would be here together when we were teenagers. We never fought over a boy. Well, not because we wanted to date the same one. We fought over her going after Thad when he broke my heart. Then we fought over the man who broke her heart. But she was there with me when I delivered Skyler. I secretly flew back up here to be with her when her parents died. She flew back with me afterward, and we've been together ever since. Some idiots thought we were a couple a few times, but that was just us playing around with them and how close we are.

I grab the rocks glass with two fingers of JD in it and take a big gulp.

"How'd you know?" I laugh at her.

"I can practically see your body trembling. We got this."

"Hey, Prez," is hollered from the stairwell. All the girls have the ability to come up here. Each has their thumbprint set in the system for all the locations. The only places without unilateral access is my office in the clubhouse and each of our rooms there.

"Hey, Ginger, Frenchie, and Keys." They move up the stairs, each dressed in leather and in their styles. Keys is always low-key in leather with low heel boots and a black band T-shirt. Ginger is in black jeans with no heel boots and a tight half shirt. Frenchie is in a bustier similar to mine and River's; she's always followed our style. More tumblers hit the countertop and more bourbon is poured. I smile when I see my aunt stepping from behind them. She's in a sexy tank top and leather pants. What can I say, we like our leather. Each of them has their cuts on, and I slip mine on before I hold up my glass. They each take one and hold it up.

"I want to thank each of you for taking a chance

on me and being willing to move somewhere you've never been before. Well, most of you." I tip my glass to my aunt. She'd come to Alaska before but only for visits. "Thank you for helping make tonight a success and helping me with my family." I lift my glass, ready to take the shot.

"Before we do that, I have a toast," my aunt says and holds her glass as she takes me in. "We are not only club members but family. We go where you go. We'll fight whoever we need to for you. Let's do this."

They all say, "Hear! Hear!" And we take the shots.

After I get my boots on, we all head downstairs. I make sure both the doors to the apartment access and the shop are secured before we leave. We don't know if the person who shot my father is coming back, so we have to protect ourselves and our businesses. We move toward the fence line that separates the shop and clubhouse from the other businesses. As we walk through the gate, I tip my head at the girl manning this entrance for the night. We just prospected her into the club.

The parking lot is completely full and spilling into the diner's lot. We enter the saloon from the side entrance and head down the hallway to my office. Jinx and I stay there while the rest of the girls make their way to the main floor. I flip on all the monitors and watch the flow. The door staff, bartenders, and waitstaff are working hard. Stormy is at the bar, leading and helping where needed. The kitchen is bustling with food going out and empty plates coming back.

"Are you ready for tomorrow night?" Jinx says from her chair across from my desk.

"Yeah, I'm more ready for that than I am tonight. We'll have church in the morning to go over a plan."

"Stormy wants to prospect; she has a friend that wants too also."

"We can talk about that tomorrow."

I watch the monitors, not ready to go out there and be around everyone else. It's something I've come to understand about myself. I don't like to be in crowds. It gives me anxiety. I know where it all stems from.

Several years ago, shortly after I had Sky, I dated an older guy who was with another biker crew, Hell's Defiance MC. They sometimes would do rides with DHMC, and I was a prospect with them at the time. Brazen didn't know then that HDMC was going against the DHMC purpose, or at least my ex was. Which is to aid in the eradication of human trafficking. That's what our run is about tomorrow. Keys found someone we need to watch.

Phantom, my ex, tried to control me. Our time together was short, but it had a lasting impact on my life almost as much as my relationship with Thad. As soon as Brazen and my aunt found out he was beating me, they rescued me from his clutches. That's when Brazen took me under her wing, and I learned a lot. She sent me to self-defense training, which propelled me into learning about all kinds of fighting styles. I learned about guns and knives too. I won't ever let a man beat me again.

But I still have lingering scars. Not just the bump on my nose from Phantom breaking it or the cigarette burns that are now covered with tattoos. I've had a few panic attacks when I'm in crowds. I have to get over them though, so I push myself. Tonight, with my nerves already close to the surface, isn't a night to push my limits.

I sit in my office watching monitors as I run the books and check over everything. I send an email to Brazen and then one to another contact of mine, Scarlett, to see if she wants to come for a visit. Jinx comes and goes, along with the other girls. None of them want to leave me for long and I'm okay with that. I don't want to be alone.

I look up at the monitors and everything changes in a heartbeat.

She's on my property and I won't have that. I know she and Thad didn't end up together and she lied about a lot of things. But I won't allow her to be here. She's only out there to cause issues. She's a bully and isn't happy unless she's putting others down.

I watch the monitors closely and see her giving the server issues. When Stormy is called over to handle it, she puts a hand up in her face. She didn't just do that to one of my employees. The server, who is a bigger girl that likes to dress retro rockabilly, is sweet and nice. She doesn't deserve to be treated like crap.

I stand up fast and so does Keys. She looks at me with questions in her eyes. She was working on her laptop and didn't see the confrontation. Besides, to her it wouldn't have looked like anything out of the ordinary. But I know the difference. The good thing is she has my back, always.

"Prez, what's up?" She looks at the monitors behind me.

"I have some trash to throw out." I grit my teeth as I move from the room. My office is right off the main floor. I stick to the perimeter of the crowd as the local rock band plays on. All my crew flanks me by the time I reach the bar where Stormy is now standing.

"Scout, you don't want to go over there." Stormy knows who I'm here for. "She's had too much to drink. I cut her off, but others continue to supply her. Harley called the police already, and I'll have Ginger or one of the bouncers escort her out."

I can't hide the grin that stretches across my face. I've wanted to kick this bitch's ass more than anyone else's. Oh, I'd love to get my hands on Phantom and show him he can't hurt me, but this bitch was a burr in my side when I was in high school. What makes this even better is that she is surrounded by the same former cheerleaders who were a part of her mean girl crew.

As I move through the crowds toward my target, people move aside like a parting of the Red Sea. She has her back to me, but the rest of her crew eyes me warily as I approach. I'm fairly certain they don't know who I am. None of them look at me with familiarity.

"Monica, you've had too much to drink," I say loud enough to be heard over the thumping bass of the rock music.

Her body straightens and her shoulders pull back. She slowly stands in her low heels and turns. She's about my height with me in my high-ass-heeled boots. Her eyes move up and down my body, taking me in.

"Well, if it isn't the grease monkey, Scout," she sneers. She thinks it's an insult, but the true insult here is that she paid to look like she does. She obviously had a few botched plastic surgery jobs. Her fake boobs don't look good. The skin around her face is pulled tight and doesn't move when her full lips do. She's dressed in tiny black faux leather shorts that barely cover her hoochie. Her top drops to one side and is open across her back. She used to call me a whore, and this is how she dresses to go out. It's pretty obvious what she wants.

"Yikes," Ginger says from behind me. I don't turn around or take my eyes off Monica.

You never turn your back on a snake.

"Scoot along, Scout, this place is for the grownups, not a girl pretending to be a boy." She looks over my shoulder. "Well, well, did you and Stream finally come out as a couple." She laughs, but none of her friends join in.

"You're in my bar. You've harassed my staff—"

"What do you mean? Virginia is just fine. She needs to get over her bullshit." Monica uses Stormy's real name.

"Stormy is my manager. But I'm also talking about your server, Justine." I point to where Justine is standing. "Don't interrupt me again." I lean forward and get in her face. "Pack your shit and get the fuck out of my bar." I'm not playing games. I should have stood up to her a long time ago. She made me miserable when I was a teenager.

"Well, I'm not giving you a good Yelp review," Monica says.

"I couldn't care less about your review. You are trash and always have been. If you're not cutting other people down to make yourself feel better, than you're just being a cunt."

"Fuck you, bitch. I'm going to win in the end. Thad and I have been together for months now." She spits in my face. I reach up and wipe her spittle away slowly.

Oh no she didn't.

I step back. I don't want to get into this with a bar full of people and police on their way. Plus, with the run tomorrow, I can't get into trouble.

"Still a chickenshit, I see," she slurs as she advances on me.

"I'm not scared of you. I'm worried all that filler in your lips is going to burst if I hit you back." I can't help the parting words. I take another step back as she continues to advance on me. Little does she realize I'm leading her toward the exit.

She pulls her hand back to slap me. But I'm ready for the move and catch it. I spin her around and raise her arm up her back. A small yank and I could really hurt her, but I don't want to do that. I'm going to be the bigger person here. She throws her head back, and I grab a handful of her hair and push her head forward before she can nail me in the face. She's bent over and I have complete control. I march her the rest of the way to the exit and push her out the door and off the deck. People are laughing and taking pictures and videos with their cell phones. This is going to be all over social media before the night is out.

"Go home and sober up before I ban you forever from the premises. And lay off the plastic surgery. No guy wants to fuck a blow-up doll, not even Thad," I bark as I push her off the porch and right into the waiting troopers. She screams, and they nod at me as they take her to their cars.

I see him standing there. He saw and heard everything.

Giving him my back, I turn and face the crowd waiting to come in. "Looks like there's more room. Enjoy yourselves, but don't make me throw you out too."

I move back through the bar and stop in front of Stormy.

"Next time let me know before it gets that far out of control."

She nods in response, but I notice her attention isn't on me. I glance over my shoulder and see he followed me in. I head for the office so I can avoid him.

I don't want to know why he's here. I don't want to hear that he's still sleeping with her.

I reach for the door to slam it shut, but it stops. In he walks, shutting the door behind him and clicking the lock into place.

"You really think I'm fucking her?" he says.

I stand my ground. I'm ready for this. I'm ready to get into this shit with him.

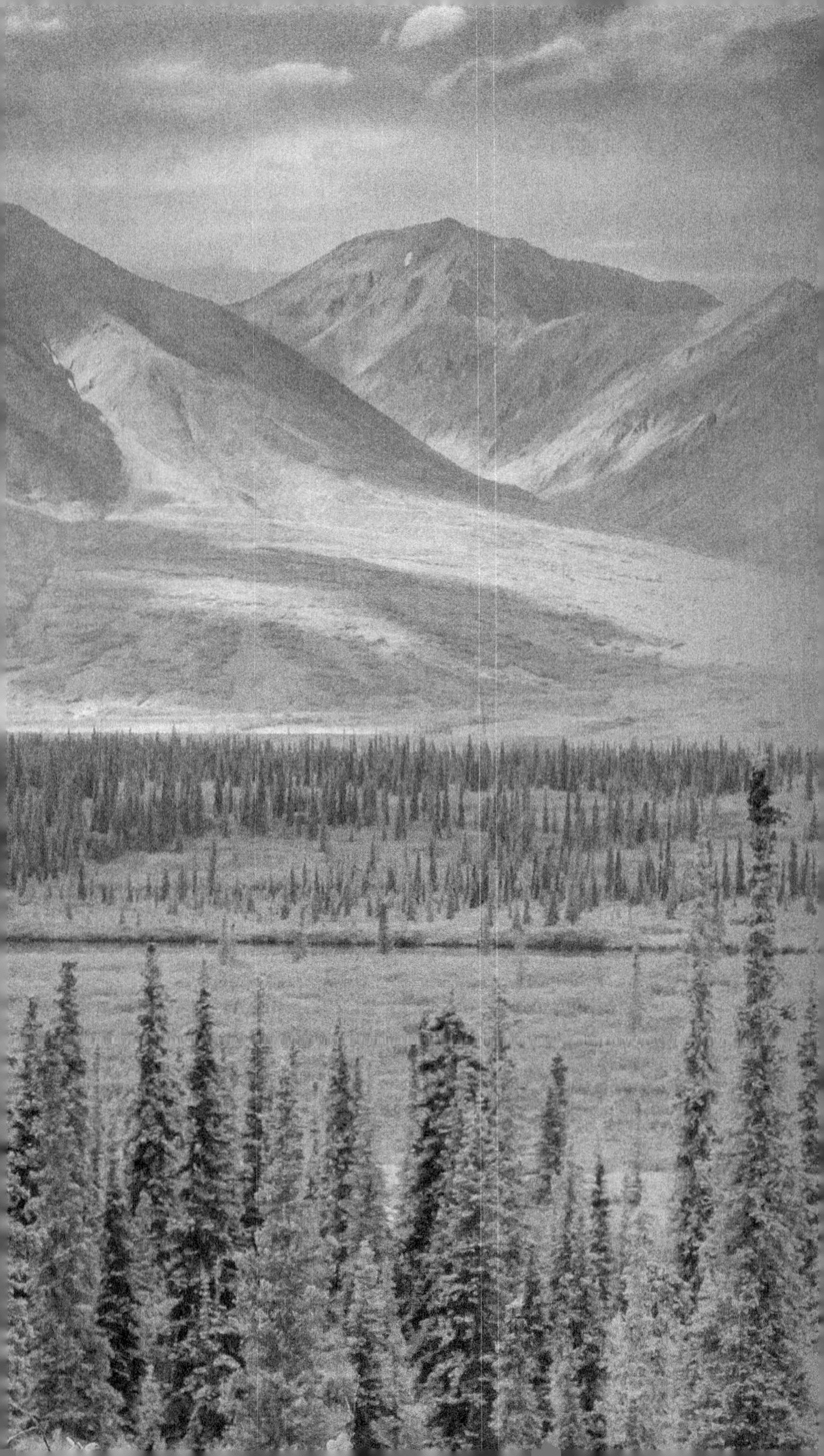

FOUR
THAD

I didn't want to come out here, but my sister said I had to see the changes Scout made to the place. I don't want to see her again. I've finally decided to put her in my past once and for all, but I still can't stop myself from wanting her. My body craves her like it does my next breath.

So, with a night off and Ryder with my mom, I decided to make the drive.

The first thing I notice when I pull up are the marked cars and troopers standing by the entrance. She sure made changes. I smirk until the doors open and I watch her push Monica out. Scout has a grip on her arm and one in her hair. She isn't even struggling, while Monica is fighting like crazy to break free.

Scout pushes Monica off the porch with a parting shot. "No guy wants to fuck a blow-up doll, not even Thad."

Her words stop me for a moment. Where would she get the impression I was fucking Monica? I glance at my ex. It's not surprising Monica would say something about us.

All lies.

I turn my attention back to Scout as she walks back inside. I follow her in, watching as she moves through the bar. I don't take in anything around me. My sister tries to stop me, but I sidestep her. I'm on a mission. I'm going to get this taken care of. Now. My eyes roam over her sexy heart-shaped ass in those tight as fuck leather pants. Her hair is shorter than when I last saw her at the funeral. The style is sexy on her. She's got her cut on over a bustier, and her very real boobs are threatening to spill out of it. Her once trim body is now curvy and demands attention.

The door to the office swings shut, but I catch it at the last second and step inside. I have something I need to do before we get into this. Her sexy as fuck body is going to be pressed up against mine. I lock the door so we're not interrupted.

"You really think I'm fucking her?" I growl as she glares at me. She's ready for a fight, and I can't stop myself. I grab her hips and lift her up. I turn and slam her back against the door. My lips are on hers before she can get a word in.

There is only one woman I want to fuck. One woman who haunts me day and night. One woman I've compared all others to.

Her mouth opens and my tongue slides in, dominating hers. This isn't like the sweet kisses we used to exchange as teenagers. This is hurt, hate, and desire rolled into one. Our teeth clash. Our tongues fight for dominance. But we don't stop. Her hands are in my hair and mine are gripping her ass, pulling her into me tighter. My cock wants to stuff her full. She was always so fucking tight, even after I took her virginity. Is she still? That thought is like a bucket of ice-cold water poured over me.

I step back and nearly drop her, but she's ready and catches herself.

Both of us are out of breath. Her tongue darts out and licks her swollen, red-stained lips. I lick my own, getting another taste of her.

"I want you." The words rip from me. I can't stop them if I wanted to. "But I know we can't."

She slowly shakes her head.

"I can't do that. You hurt me." She moves away from me.

"*I hurt you*. You broke my heart, Scout. You shredded everything I am." I advance on her. Her ass hits the desk and I lift her up. I push myself between her knees. "You let another man touch what is mine." Her head whips back as if she was slapped.

"You slept with her first. You put a fucking ring on it." Her eyes fill with tears, and I'm stunned by her words.

"What the fuck are you talking about? Yes, I

fucked Monica first. You know I wasn't a virgin when we met."

"No, you fucked her before you left." She pushes me away, and only because I'm stunned does she get the upper hand on me.

"The fuck you say?" I growl and come at her again, but this time she's prepared. I grab the back of her neck, and she pivots immediately, taking my hand in both of hers. I've seen the move but never had it done on me. She twists her body, rotating my hand behind my back in the process. I release her neck before she hurts me or herself. She pushes me back and I stumble as she moves to the door. She unlocks it, and it immediately opens.

"Please show Mr. Abbott out," she says to Ginger, who moves toward me. I stand up from the chair I fell into.

"We aren't done here, but I'll give you tonight. I'm coming to talk to you. Be ready." I walk toward the door with Ginger at my side as Scout moves out of the way. I stop and turn around, needing to make sure she understands something. "I haven't slept with Monica since I broke up with her before we started dating. She and my mom had tried to spread rumors. But that's all they were, lies and rumors." I take Scout in as she sits at her desk. My eyes move over her exposed skin in the cutouts on her leather pants. Then I glance at her lips swollen from mine. I zero in on the beard burn abrading her skin. Something settles deep inside me to know I marked her.

"I can't believe you'd believe it and cheat on me. You're the one who broke us. I heard you were sleeping with every man you could after I left." I watch her body tighten and then she's around the desk and in my face before I know it.

"I *broke* us. No, you fucking broke us. I was there. I saw her come out of your bedroom." She pauses, and before I can ask her what the fuck she's talking about, she continues. "Besides, I've slept with only five men in my lifetime. One of them was you. Three of them in the last five years. The other was after you shattered me. Who's the whore now?" Tears are streaming down her face, and I stand here trying to figure it all out. Nothing fits. I have no idea what she's talking about.

Scout realizes what she said, and she recovers quickly. "Ginger, show him out."

I'm escorted out of the saloon, my mind still wrapped around her words. Timelines are going through my head as I try to understand it all.

How the fuck does that make since?

I jump into my truck and head for the only person that could have lied to me.

Less than half an hour later, I'm pulling into my parents' driveway and looking around. They have a place up on the ridge looking down into the valley with a nice view of Fairbanks. I can make out

Chena Ridge in the distance and North Pole and the refinery further out. My mother likes this place because she's always thought of herself as better and bigger than everyone else. She can look down on the people along McGrath Road and Farmers Loop from up here.

"Thought you weren't coming back till morning to get Ryder," my dad says as he opens the door for me. I move past him to where I hear my mother talking to my son. I hear her telling him he's doing something wrong. I hate that she's so critical of him, he's only four years old.

"Ryder, go to your room for a bit," I tell him, and he jumps up to do it.

"Well, that was rude," my mom says as she smooths her hair and takes a seat on the sofa.

"You weren't playing with him, so don't act like I put you out. We need to talk."

My father sits on the opposite sofa next to me. I watch as my mother squirms in her seat. Since she heard Scout was back, she's asked me if I've seen her and how many times. She had to have conspired with Monica to break up Scout and me.

"What do you want to talk about?"

"Scout." It's all I say.

She flips her hair over her shoulder and sighs loudly. "Is that little whore spreading lies again? I told you it was best you got away from her." Her use of the word "whore" after hearing Scout refer to herself as that confirms my worst fear. My mother did something.

I hold up my hand to stop her.

"Tell me what happened." I lock my jaw and my body. I'm afraid I'll knock out my own mother if I don't. All these years Scout and I could have been together. We would have had kids with each other and not with other people.

"Son, she was sleeping around right after you left." My father tries to put in his two cents, and again I hold up a hand. I'm not ready to deal with him, but I will be soon.

"She will tell me." I point at my mother. "You and I will talk soon enough." I put him on warning. He leans back and waits.

She shakes her head, then lifts her chin high and looks down her nose at me. "I have nothing I wish to say. You seem to have made your mind up that I did something wrong. If you're going to listen to her lies, I'm done. I won't have you treat me this way. I'm your mother, for Christ's sake."

She stands up and lifts her chin another notch. I stand with her. I'm taller than her and look down at her.

"If I find out you had something to do with all this, I will cut you off. I won't have you be a part of mine or Ryder's lives."

My mother and I have always had a strained relationship. When I realized appearances meant more to her than loving us kids, I knew I'd never be able to compete. She's already cut off Stormy, who lives on her own now. All because she thinks Stormy is an embarrassment to her with her tattoos and colored hair.

"Ryder, let's go," I holler for my son. I'm not going to leave him here for her to guilt and manipulate like she does me. My mother is a narcissist, and my father has allowed her to get away with it all these years.

"How dare you threaten and talk to me like this. I don't deserve it." She has the audacity to look appalled. "I've sacrificed so much for you. Do you know I had a perfect body until you came along?" She waves her hand up and down her body. I ignore her because I've heard this too many times. Poor Stormy has been called fat by our own mother because she has curves.

"Ready, Daddy," my son says as he moves toward me, trying to get his *Paw Patrol* backpack on. I squat down and help him into it, then lift him up into my arms.

"You can't take my grandson from me." She doesn't stop, she thinks she can manipulate my son.

"Ryder, go outside." I set him down. He doesn't question but does as I ask. I watch to make sure he's standing beside the truck.

"Thad, please let him stay," my father begs. He really wants to spend time with Ryder, but my mother doesn't. He's a nuisance to her most days. He gets in her way and is a reminder that she is getting old. She doesn't want anyone to know she's a grandma and doesn't let Ryder call her that. He calls her G-ma.

A sick thought almost makes me curl over in pain. What if Scout's daughter is mine?

"Dad, this is for the best." I almost choke as I try to wrap my head around the thought of Skyler being mine. I haven't seen her up close, so I don't know. If I think about the math, it could be true. But would Scout have kept my daughter from me? I step outside and off the porch. I turn back to see my mother standing in the doorway and it hits me. She would if my mother had convinced her to.

I help Ryder up into his car seat and buckle him in. I try not to let this train of thought continue.

Later, as I make sure the blackout curtains cover the window so I can get some rest, I lie in bed and the kiss comes back to me. I look up at the ceiling of the cabin that was a dream of hers and mine to one day have. I might've pushed her out of my life, but she was always there. It's not in Ptarmigan Falls, but I'm close in the Goldstream Valley on a ridge looking out clear to the north. And that kiss still keeps playing in my mind.

Her perfect lips that I haven't sipped from in years can still make me feel like I'm free falling to earth. The first time I had to do a jump in the military it was the same feeling I got when I kissed Scout.

The thought of her sexy mouth with that full bottom lip wrapped around my cock has me hard as a rock. I just jerked off in the shower thinking about her. I roll over and try to think of anything else to get control of myself.

"Thad, just like that." Scout sighs in my ear. My cock is buried deep in her. I can feel everything. Every ripple, every spasm that she has. I reach up her back and grab her shoulder. My fingers wrap over the top and I pull her down harder onto my cock as she rides me in the front of her father's classic pickup. He'd have my balls if he knew what we were doing.

Scout rocks her hips and her clit rubs against me. Her head falls back, and I lean forward and bite along her neck. Her beautiful skin is flushed as she gets ready to orgasm.

"Sunshine, come on my cock," I growl as she lifts up and drops back down.

I pull her down harder and she blasts apart. Her body locking up around my cock. She cries out and I'm on the edge. I pull her up and down on me as I tunnel through her tightness. It feels like she's going to break my cock off, she's so tight, but I don't stop. When I finally come, I'm so deep inside her it feels like her cervix is right there and that's when realization hits me. We forgot a condom. I pull her up and off fast, but I've already started coming inside her.

"Fuck, Sunshine, I'm so sorry. I just needed in you so bad." I lean my forehead against hers as we both get our breathing under control. "You know I love you and if something comes from this, I'll make it right." I lean in and kiss

her deeply, taking her mouth so hard I know I'm going to bruise her lips.

When I finally pull away, she's smiling at me. "I love you too, Thad, and I know. It should be okay though."

I come awake and find myself covered in cum like a fucking teenager. I get out of bed to clean myself up. The dream, the memory, still lingers in my mind. Now that the seed has been planted, I wonder.

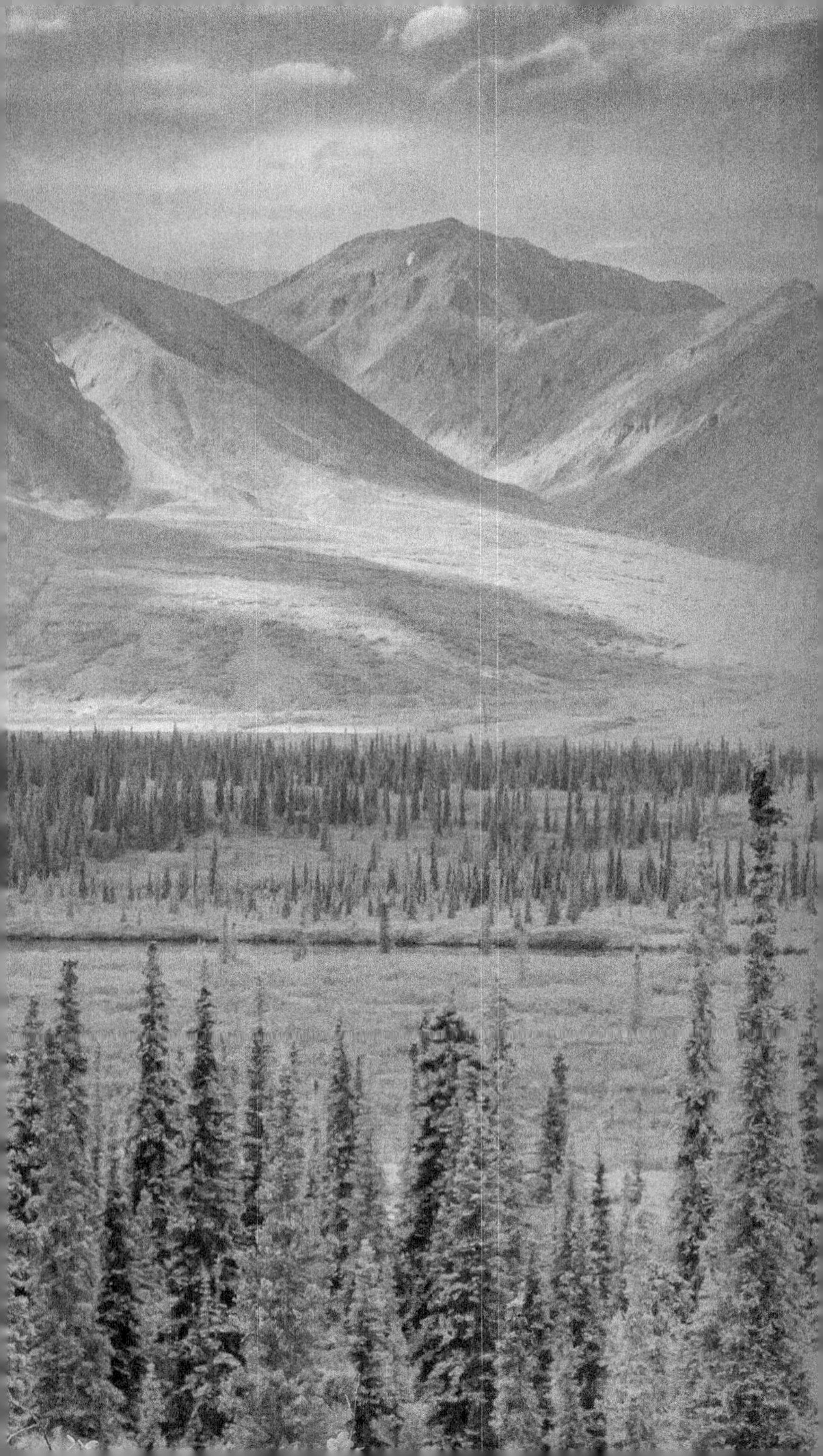

FIVE
SCOUT

The bike rumbles between my legs, not helping the state of my body. I was bad before, but since that kiss last night it's been much worse. I woke up orgasming at a memory from the last time he made love to me in my father's truck. The night we conceived Sky.

I need to get my head around this shit. We have a run tonight. I head into Fairbanks to grab some supplies. I pull into the area the locals call Little Anchorage because of the big box stores and the look of actual Anchorage. I could have driven my truck, but I needed the feel of my bike.

I have a couple of them now. When I first prospected, I had this classic Indian Scout that I've since completely restored. I got the bike because an old man took pity on me. He knew I wanted and needed a bike and knew I would love it more than his nephew. I've loved it so much and worked hard to make it what it is now. The leather seat cups my ass perfectly. Other than the paint job, it was the most expensive thing I redid. I wanted the brown leather to look just like it would have originally, but I also wanted it to be comfortable. A girl's ass isn't like a guy's. So, it took some time and money.

People move around me in the hardware store and do a double take when they see me. I'm used to my cut causing a stir, but this is completely different. Some of them grew up here and know who I am. I was notorious when I cheated on the mayor's son. Well, that was the rumor at least. I had asked River to help perpetuate it more because I didn't want his family to know otherwise after what his mother did to me.

I take my items to the register and the clerk looks at me and my cut. When she looks me in the eye, I recognize her. She went to Lathrop too. I take a deep breath and pull my wallet from the inside of my heavy leather jacket. I flip it open and there sits the reason for everything. I move the ratty threadbare piece of paper aside and grab the bills I need in order to pay.

"Aren't you Scout Keller?" the woman asks, and I huff as I nod.

"Last time I checked." I'm waiting for her to say it.

"I'm sorry about your dad," she says instead, and it takes me aback for a moment.

"Thank you."

"He was always nice when he came in."

I give her a soft smile, my lips tipping up slightly. But I keep my eyes soft too so that it seems genuine.

When I head outside toward my bike, I think for a moment. Maybe I'm the one holding on to the past and not everyone else.

"You whore," a voice I knew I'd never forget yells.

Guess I was wrong. There are still people in this small fucking town who hate me. She storms toward me in her high heels and tailored outfit. She's way too overdressed to be in Fairbanks. Her outfit is better fit for Los Angeles or New York City, not here.

"Well, hello, Cheryl." I step off the curb and walk toward where I parked my bike.

"What did you say to my son? He came to my house and yelled at me last night."

I scoff at her and grab my brain bucket helmet. She doesn't deserve anything from me.

"Didn't say shit." I get on my bike and start it up. The pipes make it loud, drowning out anything else she says. I pull out of the parking spot and take off, leaving her fuming behind me.

"Let's call this meeting to order," Jinx says from her seat to my left. The seat to my right is currently empty and will be where my sergeant at arms will sit when she gets here. I look up from the large wooden table with green and black epoxy flowing through the cracks and against the knots of the wood. It's like a river of emerald and onyx. I can't believe my father had this made in the colors of the Devil's Handmaidens for us.

"Before we get to business about tonight, let's talk members. Rivet is on her way and will be taking the sergeant position. I emailed Scarlett to see if she wanted to come hang out for a bit. She'd be perfect as a road captain. Thoughts?"

"I place a motion that we accept Rivet as sergeant at arms," Jinx offers.

As president I can't make motions or vote on them, but I can at least let my thoughts be known. I can only vote if it's to break a tie. Jinx and I are usually of one mind, so I don't have to worry about that.

Everyone agrees to the motion. I never doubted it.

"It's been brought to my attention that both Stormy and a friend of hers, Avery, would like to prospect to the Handmaidens," Jinx says, and I look around wondering if anyone is going to object. But they don't and it's decided that they will be prospects. They even come up with a road name for Stormy and I like it. As for Avery, I meet with her tomorrow. She works six days a week. She works part-time at a tattoo parlor and the other time as a night auditor for one of the local hotels.

"I received a call right before this meeting," Jinx says. I remember her getting the call, but I was focused on the email I got from Rivet saying she might be early. She was leaving Washington earlier than she thought. "The coalition would like me to ride for them next weekend at the races. Their rider was hurt yesterday and can't make the run for them. It's the debut of this bike and they want it shown with a rider. I'm not gaining points for them because they can't switch drivers mid-season, but I can ride the bike to demonstrate it."

I look around the table. I have my own reservations, but I wait. As I expected, Keys speaks up first.

"Why you? What's in it for us and the club? Besides, you haven't ridden in a while. Are you ready to do that? And, last but not least, can I run the system and double-check it? I'm not going to have you demonstrating a motorcycle that could be a bomb between your legs."

"I agree," Ginger says, and I nod.

Jinx looks at me. "Do you agree?"

If I said I didn't want her to do it, she wouldn't. But I know she likes the thrill of drag bike racing. She stopped last fall and hasn't done it since. No test in tune. No practice. No talking about it. I know why, but it's not my place to tell her story.

"I do. With everything but mostly the last two points. I want you to be sure you're ready."

"I'll call back and find out if you can do that, Keys. As for what we'd get, having a favor with them is important. They chose me because they heard I raced back in Kentucky at the wake. It gets my name out there so that we can do our own bike and start racing again," she says to everyone else. When she turns back to look at me, I see it in her eyes. "I'm ready to move on."

Her racing bike is one of the things we left back in Kentucky. I had that fine-tuned to perfection. But because we didn't own it, we couldn't bring it. I've already been thinking about getting one together for us here. It was a passion I loved to do down there. It was something she loved too.

There isn't a regular local track here, but they do allow us to race on the base runway for special occasions. In Palmer there is a track that is circle and drag. We just need the drag one, and it's only a six-hour drive for us.

"As president, I have to say I agree with the thought of always having a favor in the back pocket with them."

"Me too," both Keys and Ginger say.

"What do you say, Vixen and Frenchie?" Jinx looks at them.

"I'm worried and think only if Keys gets to run the system through her laptop. We don't want to lose you," my aunt offers.

Drag bikes can be highly dangerous if they are tuned incorrectly.

"I'm still new to the voting. I agree that favors are good, but I'm going to reserve my vote until I know if they will let Keys run a diagnostic on it," Frenchie says in her soft voice as she looks up from the notes she's taking on her laptop.

"I think we should approach Justine about

prospecting." I put the suggestion out there and they all mull it over. "Okay, laptop away," I order Frenchie, who shuts it down. Keys pulls out her laptop. After a few clicks, images pop up on the large screen on the wall.

"This is what I have." She shows us an image of a guy who looks ordinary. I mean, I wouldn't kick him out of bed. Until she pulls up the next image. "He's been grooming this young girl." The girl can't be more than fourteen. "She's supposed to be meeting him in a couple of hours at the end of South Cushman. I've looked. There are a few businesses, access to the river, and a shooting range down there."

"It's no man's land after nine o'clock at night. The parties that used to happen down there were always talked about," Jinx says, and I remember them too.

"It's too dangerous for her. Even though it doesn't get dark, she is still tempting men when she shows up there alone," I add.

"That's my thoughts. I didn't know about the IRL meetup until just a bit ago."

"Okay, Jinx and I will ride down there and check it out. Ginger, I want you and Vixen to wait at Van Horn. Keys, you and Frenchie are in my truck so we can bring her home. Everyone arm up. We roll out in an hour." I wait to see if anyone has anything to add. When there are no further questions, I stand and move out of the room. We never take our cell phones in there with us. Some lessons are learned the hard way and we don't want anyone to be tempted. The notes taken by Frenchie are just general business, and she shuts her laptop off before we get into the nitty gritty. Only Keys will have her computer in the room when church is going on. I step into the large great room filled with couches, pool tables, and enough furniture to accommodate people when we have parties here. My office is down the hall behind a fire door and across from the kitchen. As I move toward it, I dial my mom's number.

"Hey, Mom, you got Little Bear for a while?" I ask as soon as she answers.

"How long?" She knew we had business, but because she's not a part of the club, I can't tell her more. She's been wanting to join, but I keep pushing her off. I need someone to be there for Sky if something ever happens to me.

That thought is chased on its heels by thoughts of Thad. He yelled at his mom. I don't know how much of that to trust, but I do know he must have confronted her. I knew my slipup last night wouldn't go unnoticed. I must keep him at bay for a bit longer. I still haven't told my mother the truth about Sky's father.

I look at my watch and think it through in my head. "How about you bring her home in the morning and we spend the day together? I'll cook dinner." It's time I told her.

"Sure, sounds good. She's having fun. I'm teaching her to bake."

"Good, you know I never was able to conquer that one."

I hang up after talking to Sky for a bit and telling her I love her. Before every mission like this, I have to call her. I don't want her to ever doubt that I love her. I'd give up everything for her.

Once in the office, I pull the correct books on the shelves for it to slide open and reveal the gun safe behind. We can arm up, but we don't want to draw unsavory eyes, so I leave the shotgun that can holster to my other bike. I'm not going to ride my Indian. It's a wonderful riding bike, but it's also a bit showy and I don't want to stick out more than women on bikes do. I'll ride my Dyna Fat Bob instead. I grab the Springfield .45 that was my father's and then a shoulder holster. I have my pancake holster at my back and always have a piece there when I can. It's the first gun I bought myself, a Springfield XD-M .40 compact, and I've loved it ever since. It's the perfect amount of firepower for me as a personal conceal and carry.

After double-checking all my gear, I grab my full-face helmet. It will make it so I'm not recognized and I'll be able to communicate with everyone else via the Bluetooth connection. Moving to the back of the garage where my personal vehicles are kept, I open the door for my motorcycles and look at the machines in there. Not only do I have the two motorcycles, but I have a dirt bike too for playing around.

I'm not rich, but I made enough money back in Kentucky between being a race car mechanic and my business that Sky and I are taken care of. Then there is my inheritance from my father that's just sitting in the bank accruing interest. Running these businesses will be enough for us to live off of. Sky and I don't need much, but I love my toys and she has her special things she likes. She loves to ride motorcycles too and has been for a couple of years. Her small bike is sitting in the corner. But she has a thing for clothes and dolls. She's nine, I'll give her that.

I push my flat black Fat Bob out and lock up the garage as Jinx pulls hers out of her garage. She has a classic car sitting in there that was her father's. She thought it was sold after he died. She didn't know my dad had it stored for her. I can't wait until she takes it out and goes riding in it.

We all mount up on our bikes. The current prospects stay here to watch over everything on the property. They aren't ready for a mission like this yet. I have to work with them first. Frenchie is still learning some fighting techniques and hates to do it, that's why she's in the truck with Keys. Keys is in the truck because she's running the computer and monitoring emergency services to make sure we don't get caught.

We make it into town, and I head for the South Cushman area. It's still a part of town that is scary in the daylight, but I'm not afraid. I move past the old strip joints that have now moved to other areas of town. As we get to Van Horn Road that intersects South Cushman, Vixen and Ginger break off from us. Ginger wanted to be with me, but I told her I needed her out here in case the guy got away from us.

"He should be driving a Chevy Cobalt," Keys says through the comms.

I'm sweating and wishing I had the wind in my face, but this is the safest for us. All of us have our faces covered. They'll know we are women but not what we look like. Even Jinx has her long hair pulled back into a wide leather wrap and braided back.

"Oh yeah, he's a real creeper in that," Ginger says, and everyone chuckles.

We drop off the pavement at the end of the road, and I direct Jinx to the side where the gun range is. I hear guns going off and figure we won't look strange if we are stopped here.

"Heads up. He's coming."

Jinx and I stay straddling our bikes as we wait for the small car to show up. He pulls into the river access area.

"I'm going to walk that way. Jinx has our bikes." I keep my helmet on but lift the full-face part so I don't look too strange walking around with my helmet on. I'll hide my face if someone shows up.

"I think this is her," Keys says again, and I run back to my bike. "She's on her bicycle for fuck's sake."

"He's waiting. There are a few teenagers hanging out partying on the river. We might need you, Keys, to come racing down here acting like an undercover to get them to run after we grab them if it gets too dicey."

"She thinks she's meeting the love of her life, don't forget," Frenchie says. This similar scam was used on her. She was groomed by an older man who was pretending to be a teenager. She was kidnapped and taken to an auction where she was sold to a very rich man. We interfered and stole her from him. He was pissed and threatened revenge until his little secret about little girls came out.

Now we have to deal with this asshole. We start up our bikes and move over to the area. We sit and look like we are hanging back from the teenagers partying. I can still hear the gunshots from the range carrying across the partially treed area. Every shot causes my adrenaline to pump faster through my veins, but I'm also extremely calm. A deadly calm that I mastered over the years. I want to end this guy for what he's doing, but I get a rush out of it too.

Jinx nods next to me. I turn to see the girl ride her bike into the pit, and we wait to see what happens. She's looking for a Justin Bieber wannabe, not the dude in the car. She stands off to the side. Even from this distance, I can see her shaking. I slip off my bike and Jinx does the same.

We move forward as a team. The guy gets out of his car and approaches the girl. She tries to step back, but he grabs her arm. I'm on him before he knows what's happening. The teenagers are either not watching us or don't care.

"You're going to want to let her go." My voice sounds gruffer through the helmet.

"She's my sister," he lies.

I watch as Jinx takes the girl's arm and says something to her. The girl shakes her head no.

"Lie. Dude, you're on a roll tonight." He turns toward me, and I drop down into a spin, taking his legs out. He falls to the ground. "She's not yours to take."

"You can't have her," he yells, and I hit him a couple of times as he tries to stand. He falls back to the ground with his nose broken. If I hit it at the right angle, he'd be dead, but I don't want that. He'll be taken care of. His hard drive has already been copied.

"Stop poaching little girls, or I'll finish you off," I bark.

My truck pulls up and they get her and her bike into it.

I hit him again a few more times before I move back to my bike. I didn't even have to pull any of my guns. I almost snap my fingers in an aw-shucks move, but I don't let my guard down yet.

"Send the package, Keys." I give the order for her to send the evidence to the police. He doesn't have a description of me and won't be able to turn me in. Plus, he'd be implementing himself in attempted kidnapping if he ever confessed to what happened here. I'm straddling my bike, about to fire it up, when I see a teenager running toward me. I jump off, ready to defend us, when he skids to a stop.

"Hey, thanks for dealing with him. He's been coming down here every few months. Did you help the last girl?" His words cause me to freeze up. There have been more? "Last month there was another guy with him that took that girl right away. He was all tattooed and had a bike vest on too." I slip off the blood covered gloves from the beating I gave the guy and pull out a card. It just has a number and nothing else on it.

"Use this. Call and give his description. Say Riddler sent you." He nods and walks back over to his friends. I put the gloves in my saddle bag and grab out a clean pair of riding gloves before we take off.

Jinx and I escort the truck from the front while Vixen and Ginger bring up the rear. Keys and everyone heard what the kid said, and it has me wondering. We did searches. As far as we knew, none of the one percenter clubs in the state trafficked humans. I don't care about the guns, dope, and other shit, but girls I do. Humans, I care about.

"What do you think it means?" Jinx asks the million dollar question. Someone is trafficking in flesh and I'm going to have to find out who.

"We wait until we get the description," I say, not wanting to jump to conclusions.

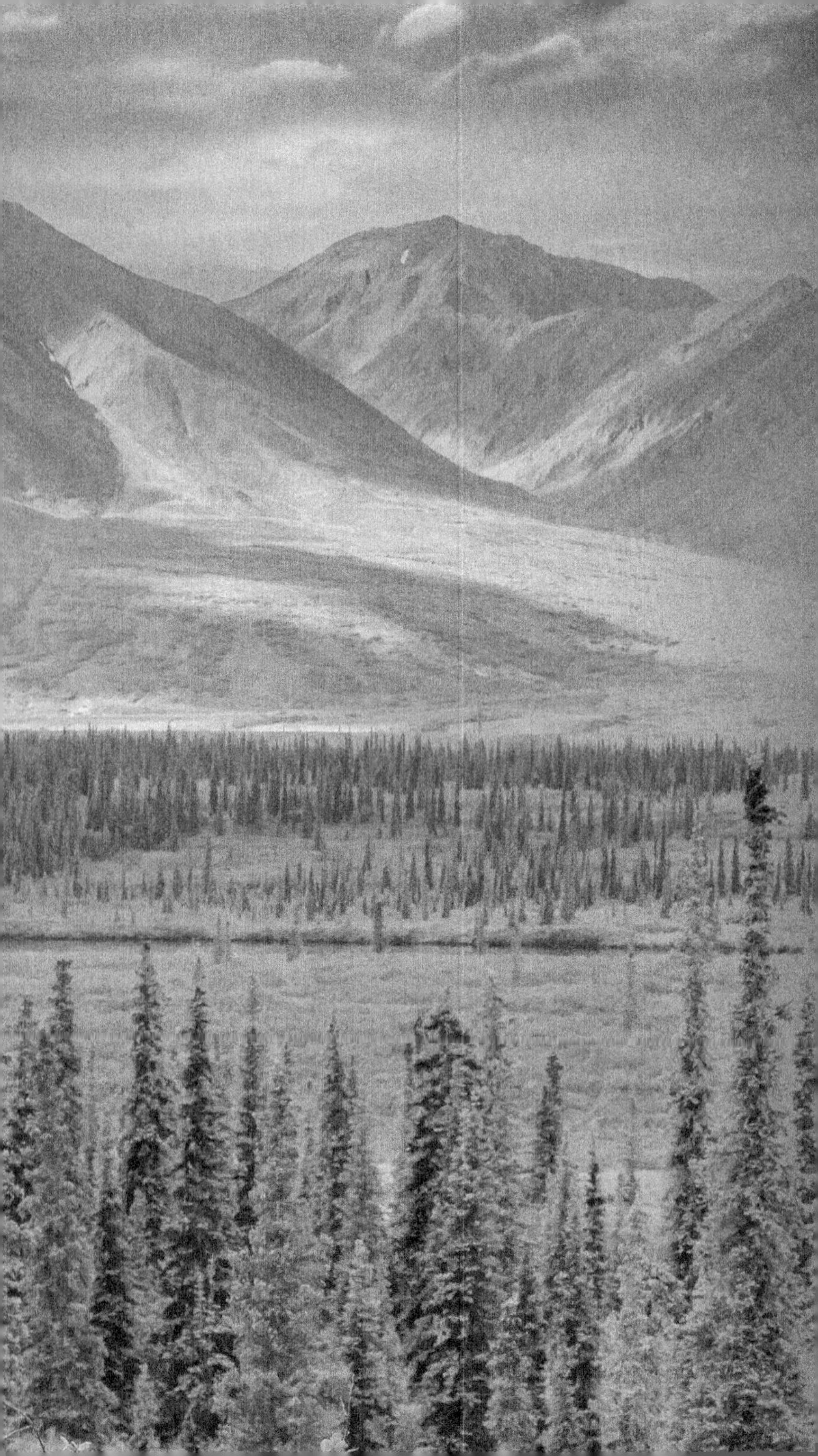

SIX
SCOUT

Last night went better than planned, except for the revelation that another club might be going against us. The coalition knew what we represent and agreed to allow us to come here and start our club chapter. We have all the approvals, thanks to my dad, but now we might have to go against one of them.

This morning went better than I thought it would too. My mom was all like "I knew it." If she knew it so much, why didn't she say something before now? Why did she make me tell her instead. When I asked her, she said it was my place to get it right.

I look over to see Frenchie and Sky playing on the jungle gym my father had built for his princess. There's even a castle. I continue walking toward the clubhouse and enter through the side door. Every door once locked down can only be opened by patches via their fingerprint. I move toward my office and take a seat behind the large desk. When I fire up the computer, I notice that Keys has already gotten a call from the kid. There were no visible patches on the guy's vest, which means he covered them. The description sounds like it could be many men. But the kid said he had a friend who got a closer look and there was a tattoo on the back of his hand. It's not a lot, but it could help.

"Ready for us?" Stormy's voice comes from the doorway.

"Come on in." I smile at them both and shake hands with Avery. I hug Stormy.

"Friday was crazy," Stormy says as they both take seats across from me.

"Yeah, it was. I didn't want to fight with her, but I wasn't going to let her treat you or any of the other staff bad."

"She was arrested and taken in for drunk and disorderly."

"Hmm." I don't comment more.

"You know she was lying, right? She and my brother haven't been together since their junior year of high school. I wouldn't put it past my mother to try to get them back together, especially since her father is a state representative. Mother is trying to push Dad into running for governor, but he says no."

"Your dad still in politics?" I don't comment on her mother because that's what Thad said after he put his tongue down my throat. I squirm at the memory.

"No, he retired. He's just running the business and playing with Ryder when he can."

"Ryder?" I'm fairly certain I know the answer to that question, but I still have to ask.

"Thad's son from his ex-wife. She was a complete bitch. She only wanted to say she was a helicopter pilot's wife. When he told her he was retiring to become a trooper, she divorced him and took off." One question and I have more info than I needed.

"Here I am." Jinx steps into the room. I was waiting for her, that's why I was okay with the small talk.

"So, Avery and I would like to prospect. We both ride and have bikes. We know it could be a long journey." Stormy stops from her rambling and works her top lip.

"What do you want to know?" I ask.

"Do you break the law?" Stormy's question is not out of left field. Everyone knows the stories and watched *SOA*. That's what they all think we are like. Don't get me wrong, some clubs do get bad, and I know we would if we had to, but I'd rather run a clean club with honor and respect than with fear.

"Not unless we have to. Once you decide to prospect and your background check comes back, we'll talk more," I tell them. I know she's concerned about her brother.

"So, Stormy, our guru of road names has come up with yours," Jinx says, and laughs as she points to Avery. "You, she'll have to be around for a bit. She helps pick the names because you can't give yourself one, you have to earn it." They all laugh, and I just sit back and watch.

I'm trying not to let my mind drift to Thad. He's been through a lot. I never got married. Yeah, Phantom wanted me to marry him, that was what started our last fight. I told him I wouldn't marry anyone who beat me. I wouldn't be his old lady. I got a broken nose and jaw for that, among other injuries. I was close to death when my aunt and Brazen found me. Poor Sky had to come visit me in the hospital because one of my lungs was punctured from the broken rib. Thank goodness she was only two and doesn't have any memory of it, as far as I know.

"Well, what is it?" Stormy asks.

"Poison. Vixen said you come up with some mean drinks." My aunt likes to help give people their road names. She gave me and Jinx ours. She's come up with the other girls' names too.

"I like it." Stormy and Jinx are laughing, but I notice Avery isn't. She's looking around and avoiding eye contact. She's hiding something.

"Avery, why don't we talk. You can tell me why you want to be a part of the Devil's Handmaidens," I say as I look at Jinx, sure she'll understand. She grabs Poison's arm and pulls her along with her.

"But what about Avery?" Poison asks. The door is closed before Jinx answers her.

"I need help," Avery says as she starts crying. I move around the desk and sit in the seat next to her. Her long hair is stark white and deepest black. From what Poison told me before, Avery is an artist. "Is it true what they say about you?"

"I don't know what you mean?" I play dumb because until she's a prospect who has cleared a lot of hurdles does she find out what we really do. It's what keeps everyone safe.

"That you help women."

"How?" I don't clarify what I mean by that. Her answer will tell me how I'll answer her.

"I've heard from some people that the Handmaidens in the lower forty-eight save women from traffickers." Okay, I didn't expect that.

"Where did you hear that?" Not many know we do this. They know we are against it, but they don't know how we do it unless they are a part of our crew. They don't know about the numerous rescues we've been on.

"My brother runs with an MC in Anchorage, and he told me. He begged me to talk to you."

"What do you need help with?"

"Our little sister went missing. She hasn't been found and the cops are saying she's a runaway. She was in foster care because our parents aren't the best and I worked too much to have her. But she's been gone for three weeks now." She cries harder. "I'm trying to get the money together so she can come live with me. But my boss at the tattoo parlor fired me because I've been out looking for her so much. I don't know what I'm going to do."

"Just a sec." I hold up a finger and grab my cell.

>   ME
>
> Keys, need you and the laptop.

I send the message, then set my phone back on the desk. I don't need to wait for a response. She will come. I reach over and pat Avery's shoulder. When she looks up at me, I see the devastation on her face and stand so that I can hug her.

"I'm about to lose my apartment, and the state lady said I have to have an apartment by myself." Her body shudders. I continue to hold her, knowing the state doesn't make it easy for siblings to get their younger ones when they are in foster care.

"Here, Prez," Keys says from the doorway. I pull away and grab the box of Kleenex for Avery.

"Give her all the information you can on your sister and the foster parents. Keys can do some looking. I can't guarantee anything, but we can look."

"So it's true." She looks at me with hope in her eyes. I hate to dash it, but I have to be honest.

"We can only look. I can't guarantee we'll find her, but we can at least find out where she was last."

"I won't tell anyone. I promise." She turns toward Keys and gives her the information she asks for.

After they are done, Keys nods at me and leaves the room. She's got a full bank of computers at her fingertips back in her room. I need to designate an office for her soon so she can separate her place of work from relaxation. Keys has a way of letting her work rule her and she needs some downtime.

"Now, about the job and place to live. For now, I can have you work in the bar, but I'd like to get you set up doing tattoos and such out here. The girls are always wanting to get pierced or inked and don't want to go to town. Plus, I have the space to do that. Start thinking if that's something you'd like to do." It's true, I was going to call a friend to see if they wanted to come up and help me start a parlor out here. But if I can get a local, I will. I've seen her work on Poison's body. She's very talented. "As for a place, I can't offer you more than a room here. Normally, prospects don't get their own room. But we have the space, and we like to help. The state won't let your sister stay here, but if we have to, my mom is set up to foster. She got all the paperwork together years ago."

She wipes her eyes and looks across the desk at me. "You'd really do all that?"

"You are going to be family. Keys has already done a preliminary background check on you and there were no red flags. If you don't mind being a slave for a bit, you'll survive being a prospect."

I direct her out of the office as I lean back and think of what we can possibly do to help her. Keys will get as much info as possible, but Alaska is a huge state. Avery's sister could be anywhere. And with so many remote locations and not as many cameras as the lower forty-eight, it will be like looking for a needle in a haystack.

Thad

I haven't seen her since last Friday. My sister sat me down and explained why she wanted to prospect for the Devil's Handmaidens MC. I'm worried this is going to drive a bigger wedge between us. Leaving Stormy here for all the years I was in the military was hard on her. With a mother like ours, she didn't have the maternal image most young girls have. Scout's mom was motherly to Stormy, and that's why she started working at the café first then moved on to the saloon.

"Hey, Abbott, you got anything new on that murder out in Ptarmigan Falls?" My captain steps into my office.

"Still looking. Why?"

"We got a burned truck with partial plates to the ones you found on the camera. Here." He hands me a message slip from the fire investigator, and I stand up. "Some messed up paper pushing caused this to get lost in the pile. Good luck."

"I'll check it out and then I have to head down to Palmer for that extra training you wanted me to do this weekend." I'm working a partial shift today so I can get down there at a halfway decent time.

"Yeah, better hurry." He laughs as he steps out of the room.

Since my fight with my mother, I haven't taken

Ryder to her house. Stormy is working, so I'm taking him down with me. I have several friends who live in Palmer. Griffin said his wife wouldn't mind watching Ryder for me while I'm in training. I'm going to be staying at another friend of mine's place, Dylan. We met while we were in the trooper academy. He's stationed in Palmer along with Griffin.

Heading toward the call for the burned vehicle off of the backside of Badger Road between Fairbanks and Anchorage, I'm not hoping for a lot of information, but just a small bit could help. One fingerprint would be nice. The perp wore gloves in the saloon and hid from all the cameras. We were lucky to get the partial plate from the gas station across from the saloon. We caught the truck again on cameras coming into Fairbanks but lost it on the Steese obviously heading to where it is now.

The fire investigator is standing near the truck when I pull up. I called him before I left the office and let him know I was en route. I step out of my vehicle and slip my hat on my head.

"Abbott." He reaches out and shakes my hand.

"Thompson." I nod at him. "What you got?"

"1995 GMC pickup. I got some clothes and gloves in the bed. It's a good thing there has been some rain. It left some of the interior and debris in the bed of the truck from complete damage. But there has been some animal activity."

I walk over and look down at the long put out fire.

"Fire crews weren't called in?"

"They were. Put it out and got called to a bad car accident. They thought the troopers had it. You all thought fire had it. Ball got dropped. But when a neighbor called it in again because it was attracting a griz, I was called in. I called you when I did my due diligence."

I hate that this has been out here since Levi's death, but we got it now. I look into the bed and sure enough I see the clothes. I'm not hopeful, but it can't hurt. After grabbing bags from the back of my SUV, I start collecting evidence while Thompson holds a shotgun to keep the bear back if it shows up again.

I find several articles of clothing, including what looks like a small woman or teenager's clothes. I'll take them with me and get them to the lab in Anchorage while I'm in Palmer. It will be quicker than any other way right now.

"Let's have it towed for now and put in impound. I've got the owner's information and will call them too. But it was reported stolen."

"Yeah, I found that too. Let me know if you need anything else."

I leave Thompson at the site to wait for the tow truck. Normally, I'd wait, but as I'm pressed for time, I hit the road. The six-hour drive to Palmer is going to be busy with it being summer.

Ryder sleeps most of the way, even though I pull over several times to get him out and let him run around. We make it into Palmer at seven in the evening. Our first stop is to the station to drop off the evidence so it can head into Anchorage in the morning.

By the time we get to Dylan's, Ryder isn't ready to head to bed, and with the sun still up, he plays outside with Griffin's kids. Dylan doesn't have any kids, but he and Griffin live close by each other off of Lazy Mountain.

The next day, after several hours of hostage negotiation training, Dylan and I decide to head out to the Knik Bridge and Jim Creek area to show Ryder. The parking lots are full of families and others from the around the area and Anchorage who want to ride four-wheelers, dirt bikes, and other off-road vehicles. Several families camp out here too. It's a bit of a lawless area because troopers can't be out here all the time. Vehicles get burned and there is lots of drinking and drugs. Locals like to come out here too, but they hate that it's overrun by city people. This area is an access point to get to the Knik Glacier about twenty-five miles up the river.

In the distance you can hear the drag race cars at the racetrack. The sound reverberates off Pioneer Peak through this part of the valley. Pioneer Peak stands over the valley like a centaur keeping an eye on its minions below. The beauty of the rugged mountains, glaciers, and rivers keeps people visiting.

"Can we go see the cars, Daddy?" Ryder asks me

full of excitement. He's always loved cars. At almost five years old, it's either dinosaurs or cars.

"I guess we can. What do you say, Dylan?" I ask our tour guide.

"Sure, why not. They're probably only doing tests and tune at this time of night. Celebrating today's winners." He laughs as he climbs back up into his large truck. He's right, it's almost nine o'clock at night. People are still running around and playing as if it was midday.

We load up and are about to head out when a call comes across the radio in Dylan's truck. It's for a suspected assault at the Alaska Raceway Park.

"Looks like we have to go there anyway."

"I'll hang back with Ryder. You do what you need to."

We make the quick five-mile run and pull up to the pit gate entrance. The dispatcher said ambulance is on its way. Suspect is still at large but female victim is secured. We can't get too close because of all the cars, motorcycles, and campers in the area. Dylan parks and gets out. He heads to where the crowd is. Everyone parts as he walks up, and I see someone I recognize. My body instantly starts shaking. Please don't let it be her.

"Ryder, stay here, little man," I order him. I jump out and see Scout's daughter being led away from the group crying along with Scout's friend, the French one.

I move toward her, and she steps back, but the

little girl just looks up at me. Her eyes are swimming with tears, and I know in that moment it's Scout who's hurt.

"I can't remember your name, but my son is in the back seat of that truck." I point to Dylan's truck. "Can I trust you to watch him?" I ask the French woman.

"My name is Minuet or Frenchie, and yes, I'll watch him. Maybe he'll help me distract Little Bear." Her accented voice is soft as she waves to the young girl.

"Thank you." I start to move away from them when the little girl finally speaks.

"Why did someone hurt my momma?" she asks me.

I turn back around and drop to my knee in front of her. Looking at her, I see so much of Scout, but I'm too focused to really look at her. Now's not the time.

"We'll find him, Little Sunshine." I fluff her hair and she smiles at me.

"Sunshine is what my mom hates to be called," she comments with a giggle, and it takes me a moment. I stand up and start moving. People shift and I see her lying back in the bed of a truck. She's already strapped to a backboard from the racetrack's safety crew.

She looks over and sees me. I stop and take in the damage. She's in running shorts, a sports bra, and a tattered T-shirt. The safety crew is in the process of cutting the shirt the rest of the way off her.

I can't stop my legs. I'm moving closer to her when River steps in front of me.

"Get out of my way," I growl at River. She doesn't move. She puffs out her chest, ready to fight me.

"Thad, this isn't the time. I don't know why you are here, but we got this handled."

"It doesn't matter why. I'm here now and I'm going to check on her. So get the fuck out of my way." I don't look at River. I keep my eyes on Scout, who is watching me. I see the pain roll across her face every time they shift her around.

"No. She doesn't need or want you." River's words are harsh, but I finally look at her. I lean down into her space.

"I don't care what she wants. I just told her crying daughter I would help her, so get the fuck out of my way." My voice is harsher and I'm about to pick her up and move her.

"Hey, Thad, want to come help me," Dylan says, sensing that something is going on.

"You saw Skyler?" River's voice has a slight tremble in it, and she looks over her shoulder to Scout. I keep my focus on River, watching every emotion, knowing there is more going on here than what it looks like.

"Let him, River." Scout's voice has a tremble to it, and River finally steps aside. I move past her and lean into the back of the truck. Her mom is sitting next to her, hovering close.

"Sunshine, what happened?" I want to take her hands, but her knuckles are broken from fighting.

"Thad, do you know her?" We both look up at Dylan at his question.

"I do." He gives me a look, his eyebrow raising. "Long story." I don't elaborate with the crowd around us.

"Hello, I'm Trooper Dylan Butler. Can I ask you some questions about what happened here?"

"I'm Scout Keller." She cringes. "I was taking a run after the races." She coughs and tries to turn her head, and I can see the marks on her neck where someone tried to choke her. "I was on a trail alongside the road when someone attacked me from behind. He grabbed me and I tried to fight him off."

"Looks like you got in a few licks." I run a gentle finger over her knuckles.

"I don't need a hospital. I know what I'm dealing with here." She tries to push up away from the board, but the straps keep her down.

"Riddler, I found you barely conscious. Let them take you in, just in case," Ginger says.

"Gin, I'm okay. I've had worse before."

"Scout Clementine Keller, you will let them take you in," her mother barks the order.

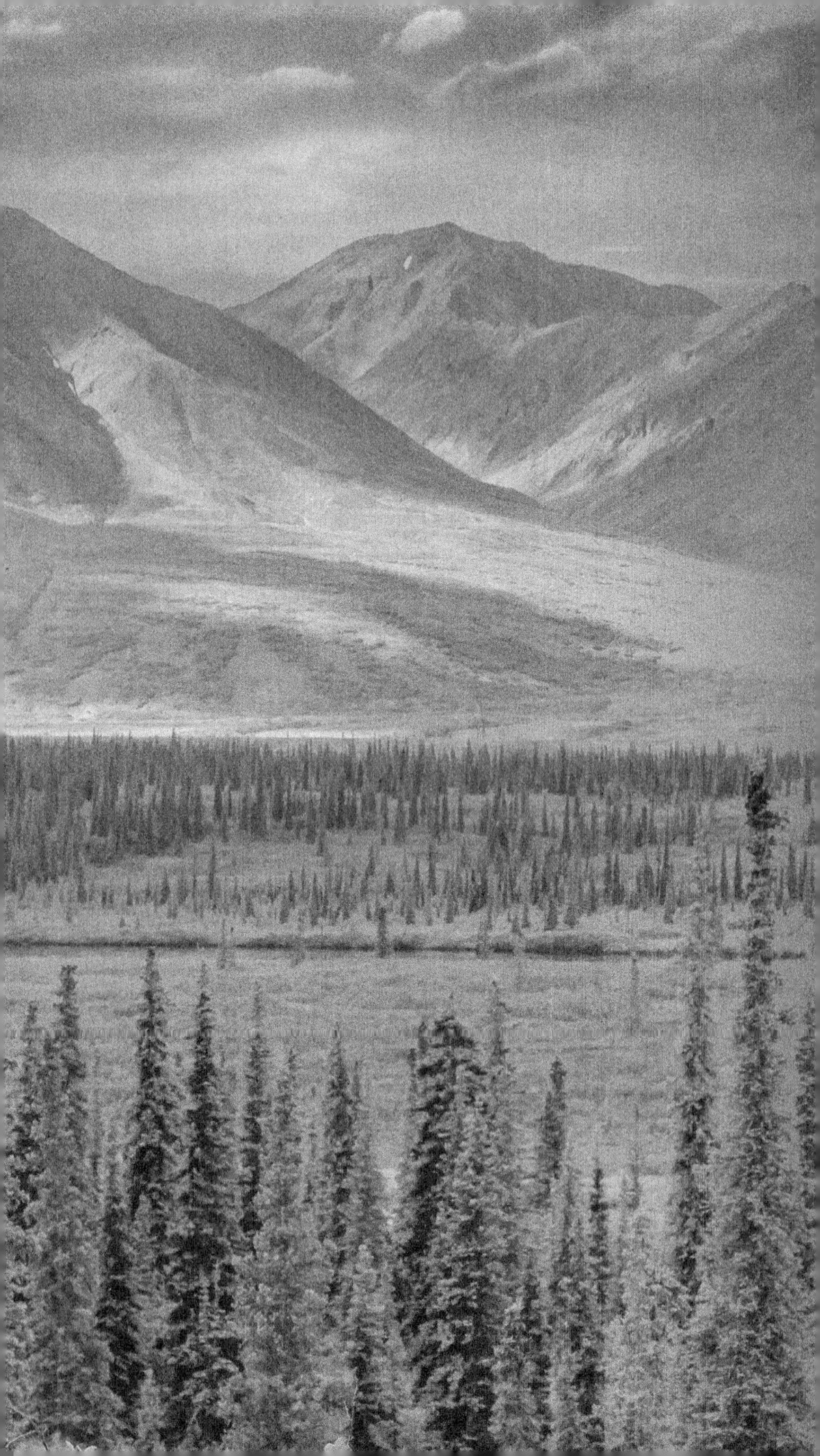

SEVEN
SCOUT

I can't believe he is standing right here. I'm freaking out. He insisted that Skyler ride with him and his friend to the hospital and follow the ambulance. He did give in and let River ride with me.

Every part of my body hurts. I've been x-rayed. CAT scanned. Now I'm lying here as we wait for the doctors to decide what they want to do next. I watch Thad though. He's pacing back and forth in front of the door.

"Are you sure about this?" River asks me softly. She's seated on a chair next to the bed. My mother is in the waiting room with Sky and Ryder, Thad's son. She was in here for a while, but the memories from before were too much and she had to walk out. She only showed up days after I was attacked last time. I was already out of the ICU, but she still saw all the damage that was done to me.

"I don't know," I answer her honestly. I'm not sure

what is going on or what I can do to make this better. Or for that matter worse. The longer he's around Skyler, he'll know the truth. That I didn't do what I was supposed to do.

"May I come in?" A deep voice comes from the doorway. I recognize the trooper, Dylan, who is working the case. He steps in and looks around the room at everyone.

"Come in," I say softly. My voice hurts every time I talk, but I know he needs to ask his questions to find out who did this to me.

"Can I ask questions with everyone here?" His question isn't surprising, but it's Thad who takes it the wrong way.

"I'm not leaving, Scout." He directs his gruff growl at me.

I've tried to get him to leave several times. When a doctor told me my nose was broken again and I shrugged and said it wasn't the first time, I thought Thad was going to come unglued.

"Who broke your nose?" Thad asks the same question he's asked several times.

I look at Dylan. That's what he told me to call him when he found out I was friends with Thad. My mother steps back in and sits next to River.

"Do you have any enemies?" His first question is a doozy. I look at my mom and then to River before I look at Thad.

Taking as deep of a breath as I can with a couple of fractured ribs, I don't look at Dylan but at Thad when

I answer. "Yes. I probably have several. However, there's only one I can think of who would get enjoyment out of beating me. But he isn't here. He's serving ten to twenty for assault in the lower forty-eight." I watch as both River and my mother stiffen, but it's Thad who is holding completely still. "My ex was put in jail for beating me up."

"Have you been notified that he's been paroled or anything?"

"No. He was supposed to serve a minimum of ten because he almost killed me. I'm supposed to be notified if he does get released. His name is Stanley Smith, but he goes by Phantom. He used to be with the Hell's Defiance Motorcycle Club. I'd heard he was excommunicated from them for other issues. I can get a hold of someone who would know for sure."

"What other issues?" Dylan asks me, and I finally look away from Thad. I'm going to lie, and he'll know.

I shake my head. "I don't know." He was kicked for trafficking in girls. He was helping by being the middleman or collector, but they never caught him for that. The only reason Phantom is in jail right now is because he beat me up.

"Almost killed you?" The growl comes from the foot of the bed, and I look down to Thad.

"He beat me when I refused to marry him or be his old lady. Broke my jaw, nose, punctured a lung. Oh, and broke my arm." I can't hide the bitterness from my tone.

"Don't forget that he was beating you before then too," my mother says, adding more fuel to the fire in Thad's eyes.

"Why did you stay with him?" Thad asks the million-dollar question.

I scoff and then cringe from the pain. "You don't want to know." I turn back to the other trooper. "Dylan, do you have more questions?" When a thought hits me, I smile as I look at Thad and then back to Dylan. "I do have two more enemies. Monica Granger and Cheryl Abbott. They've both threatened me at different points." I pause to let that bomb drop in the room before I end it. "But this wasn't either of them. I handed Monica her ass last week, and it's beneath Cheryl to get her own hands dirty. Plus, this was a man. I know even though he had a mask on. His build."

Dylan looks from me to Thad. "Abbott, as in your mother?" It's fun to see him in the hot seat. The doctor walks in.

"I need the room." Everyone but my mother and River step out. I look at the doctor and then my mom.

"I'm going to discharge you. You're going to want to follow up with an ENT specialist about the nose to make sure the septum is okay. As for the ribs and knuckles, they should heal. Your throat is going to be tender for several days. I'm giving you a note for you to take the next week off work."

"I own my own business," I interrupt him. "I'm a mechanic."

"I suggest you give your ribs and knuckles time before you start back up."

"Thanks."

"Let me get your discharge paperwork ready and then you can go."

He walks out and Thad walks back in. "May I talk to her, please?"

I'm not ready to deal with him and I need space.

"No, I'm getting changed. You can wait out in the lobby until I come out." I push him off and watch as his body straightens to his full height. He turns and walks out the door.

Thad

She's hiding things. I know she lied to Dylan. I don't know why she did. The thought that someone wanted to kill her makes my blood run cold. But what's worse is the fact she thinks my mother and Monica want her dead. There is more to what my mother did. I don't want to talk to Monica, but I guess that's going to be next on my list of trying to get this all figured out.

When I step out into the lobby that is full of her crew and friends, I shake my head and move to where my son is sitting with her daughter. This time I take her in more. She's got her mother's hair, but her eyes are a blue that is light and look familiar. I can't place them though. River walks over and stands next to me.

"Sky, let's go. Momma is about ready." The girl gets up and smiles at me. My heart clenches because I get it now. I start to get in the way and stop River from taking her when I notice Ginger and Vixen standing behind me. Security is making their way toward us too. Dylan walks over and stands next to my arm.

"Let's get Ryder out of here. I've got the information I need."

I continue to look around and watch as they take Skyler out the door. Everyone with her moves out. Scout said we'd talk, but she's running.

"Daddy, Sky said she'd come to my birthday party." Ryder gets my attention when he takes my hand.

"Okay, buddy." I bend down and pick him up, rushing to follow the group.

When I exit the hospital, I watch as Scout sits in the passenger seat of a car I don't recognize and is whisked away. I turn to look for Skyler and find she is already loaded up into Scout's truck with River driving. Everyone is leaving.

Well, I'll talk to them when I get back home. She can't run for long. Plus, this gives me time to question Monica first. Maybe I'll gain some insight into what is really going on here.

A couple of weeks later I'm sitting in the Cookie Jar waiting for Monica to show up. She wanted me to take her to dinner, and then for me to come over. But I'm sticking to being very public for many reasons. I don't think she'll cause a scene here. I decided lunch would be the best option.

I haven't gotten to talk to Scout. She's avoiding my calls. I'm going to head out there as soon as I get done with this meeting and get the information I need. I look up as I hear my name yelled. I'm sitting right where she can see me. Why the fuck is she yelling? I stand up because that's what my dad taught me, but I'm not prepared for her to plaster herself against my body and lean up for a kiss. I avoid it and carefully push her back.

I'm pretty sure this is going to come back to bite me in the ass later on.

"Let's sit, Monica." I direct her to the chair across from mine, and she continues to stand there. I take a seat. I'm not here for a date, so I don't want to pull out her chair. She huffs and finally pulls it out herself. She's dressed in jeans so tight I wonder if she was poured into them. Her top is strapless and barely covers her fake boobs. I heard that when she was arguing with Scout. There was a comment about her lips being fake too.

I don't want her to think I'm thinking of her lips, so I don't look at them.

"I'm so glad you called and wanted to get together. I think you and I are ready to finally settle down," she says, and I look at her with an eyebrow raised.

"Are you on drugs?" I can't stop the question. "I want to know what you and my mother did to Scout?"

She scoffs. "Are you kidding me? Why is it always about that bitch? Don't you know she cheated on you? Slept with some North Pole guy."

My head tips to the side and I'm about to ask her what she's talking about because that's different than anything I've heard so far, but the server walks up. Monica makes a big show of grabbing my hand and trying to take it, but I pull it back.

"Coffee and that's all," I tell the girl. I'm not eating with Monica. My stomach is rolling from the possibility I fell for lies and missed out on my daughter's life because of this bitch. I'm fairly certain Skyler is mine. Her eyes are just like mine; I know it like I know that Ryder is mine. No doubt about it.

"I'd like a diet coke, and can I also have the house salad, no dressing." Monica hands the menu to the waitress. I hand mine over and wait for her to start again, but she just sits there.

"Monica, what happened to the story about Scout cheating with an Army guy from the post?" I watch her for stress queues and other signs she's lying. When her eyes flick up to the side, I got her.

"She cheated with several men. Why do you care?"

"Do you know who Skyler's father is?"

Her eyes flick again.

"Why do you care? Who's Skyler?" Again, the eyes flick. She doesn't lie very well. I watch as she squirms in her seat, and I'm done. I lean over and she's about to reach for me. She looks around to see who's watching. "Do you have a call, my love?" she asks me in a sugary sweet voice.

"If I find out you're lying to me, I'll bury you. I'm not interested in you. Not now and haven't been since I was a stupid teenager." I walk away as she sputters and calls my name. I stop at the counter and pay for my coffee and her salad and drink, acting like I didn't just make a huge scene.

When I pull into the parking lot of Violet's café, I notice it's already closed for the day. I see the fence around the automotive business and clubhouse. I move toward the fence that is currently open because the business is open. I move to the first bay and see River walking across the back. She's in a white cover that has paint flecks all over it. She was an artist in school, and I see she's continued that to becoming an automotive paint technician.

"River," I say her name, and she turns to look at me. I watch as her eyes flick to the office area and then back to me.

"Hey, Thad." She acts like there is nothing going on.

"I need to speak to Scout."

"She's not here." She didn't have to think about it.

"Where is she? At her mom's, or does she have a place?" I watch as a woman about the same height as River walks up. She has deep brown almost black hair with full lips and a curvy figure you can see under her coveralls. I can tell she's a mechanic too because she has oil and grease on them.

"Jinx already told you Riddler isn't here. Now leave." I'm not in my uniform, so the new girl has no idea who I am. I pull out my badge and flip it open so she can see it. "So." Her eyebrows drop, and she chuckles. "That isn't going to give you the information you don't need. What do you want?"

The girl has fire and she's squaring off with me, but River steps around her and pushes her back.

"Rivet, this is Thaddeus," River says, as if that explains everything. Rivet's eyes get big and she looks me up and down. "Thad, she really isn't here. Her mom took her to an appointment."

"I have a message for her." I don't want to play this game with her, but I will if she doesn't speak to me soon. "Tell her to call me. If I haven't heard from her by next week, I'll be seeking a lawyer." I don't say anything else and leave. I can feel others watching me, and it's not until I get into my truck that I see the women standing on the porch of the clubhouse. My sister starts to move toward me. I roll down my window and she runs over.

"Thad, what are you doing?"

I know I spoke loud enough with the threat about an attorney for her to hear.

"I'm doing what I need to. I need to find out if Skyler is my daughter." She steps back from the side of the truck and drops her eyes. "You know what I'm talking about. Has she told you?"

"Thad." She shakes her head and looks up at me. She is torn between her family of choice and her family of birth. I watch as she takes a deep breath slowly in and out. "I don't know about that. I honestly don't know. But Riddler is really at an appointment with her mom."

"Poison," someone hollers, and I look up as my sister backs up more.

"I have to go." She turns and walks away from me.

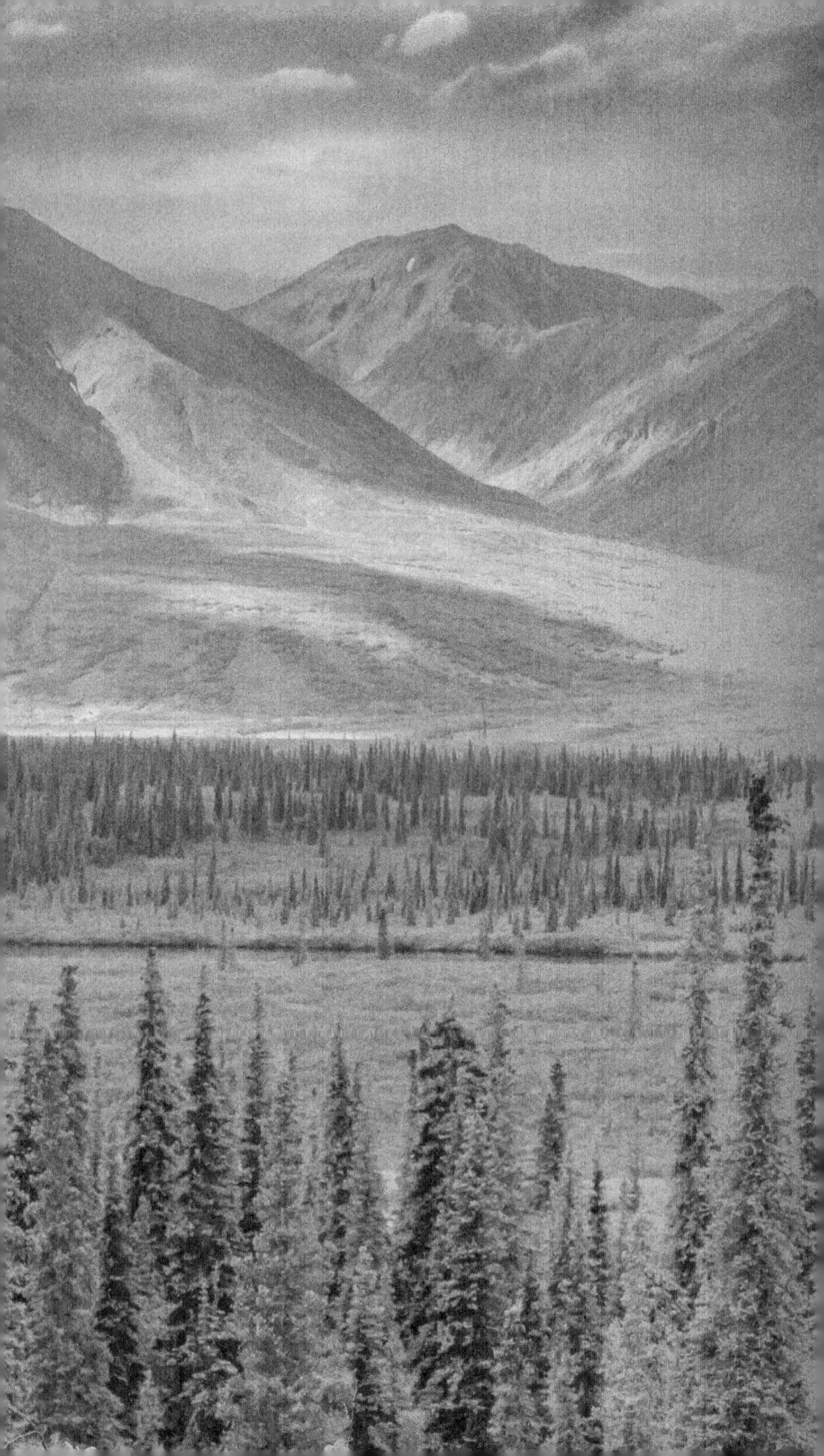

EIGHT
SCOUT

"Are you sure you want to do this?" My uncle leans heavily on his desk. My leg is bouncing up and down. I've been ignoring Thad's calls. I know he wants the truth. I can't give him all of it, but I can do this.

"Yes." I sigh deeply as I stand up. I'm still sore from the attack from a couple of weekends ago. I know that I shouldn't do it, but when I get back, I'm going to go for a ride. First, I need to get this taken care of. I need to tell my truth.

As I move out of the office, my mother stands from her seat. She and I have spent hours talking about this over the last few weeks. By tomorrow Thad will be served with the paternity paperwork. I've also included a proposed visitation schedule. I'm going to do what's right by my daughter, regardless of what they made me agree to years ago.

By the time we get back to Ptarmigan Falls, I'm a

basket case. I need a ride more than I need a shot of whiskey. I move past everyone milling around to the back of the shop and open the garage. I want something fast and nonrecognizable, so I move to the Fat Bob and gear up. I already have on a pair of riding jeans with extra padding for protection. I carefully hang my cut on a hook and grab my leather jacket. I don't want to be recognized. I just want to be me for a few moments. River and Rivet find me by the time I reach for my full-face helmet.

"He came by. I told him you were at an appointment."

"That prospect Poison was talking to him. She might've said something. Want me to question her?" Rivet barks.

I slowly shake my head. I don't want that. If she said something, it's okay. It's too late to fix this situation. It's too late to take it all back. She can't be made to choose between me and her own brother in this.

"No. First of all, she doesn't know anything to tell, and second, she can't make that choice. I don't want her to."

Rivet shakes her head, but I see the small smile on River's lips.

"Rivet, she was too young to know. She saw me though, so that's all she needs to tell him if he asks." I nod at them both before I throw my leg over the body of the bike. I sat down the girls in my inner circle and told them all the truth.

"Are you sure you're up to this?" Rivet asks. She

showed up on the Monday after the attack and has been helping me. She is concerned just like everyone else.

"I'm okay. I'll take it easy." I hit the switch and the machine comes to life. I don't take it easy as I speed out of the area and head for the one place where I feel better lately. Our spot.

I knock on the door, afraid to be here, but I need to tell him. He said he'd make it right. I know he's supposed to leave on Monday for MEPS. The door opens and Cheryl stands there.

"Yes?" she asks like she doesn't know who I am.

"I need to talk to Thad." I shuffle from foot to foot. I'm scared, but I don't look down. Something deep inside me says to keep my eye on her. I watch as her lips pinch slightly, and she starts to smile.

"Thad doesn't want to see you. He's with the real love of his life." At that moment I look over her shoulder and see Monica walking up.

"Mom, Thad wants a sandwich, can I make you one too?" Her voice is so high pitched, I bet the dogs in Delta Junction heard her.

"We-We didn't break up." I can't help the catch in my voice. "It's important." I trust him. There has to be something else going on here, but it doesn't feel like it. It feels real. I pinch myself and look around. Thad's truck is sitting in the driveway. He's here.

"He told me he dropped you because you wouldn't make a good officer's wife," Monica says, and I remember the slight disagreement we had about me being a proper

military wife. But we didn't break up. He said we'd work on it.

"No, we didn't." My chin lifts, and I'm ready to swear on a stack of bibles.

"Thad told me he was only with you to see if you'd put out. He didn't want to be with you forever. Jeez, you're so gullible." She laughs and my heart stops in my chest. *When we first started seeing each other, there was a rumor that was why he was with me.*

"My son will never marry a girl from Ptarmigan Falls. The only reason we agreed to his marriage to Monica is because of the family she comes from."

At that moment Monica holds out her left hand. Sitting on her ring finger is not only a beautiful engagement ring but the one that he tried to give me, and I told him I wasn't ready.

I am now.

It didn't take him long to move on. He said he'd wait forever. I'm still in high school.

"That can't be." I can't stop the movement as my hand goes to my lower stomach to protect my unborn baby. *Thad's unborn baby.*

A cold hand claws into my forearm and drags me into the house.

"God, I hope none of the neighbors saw that," Cheryl bites out and then drags me into a room in the house. I look around and notice I'm in an office.

"Monica, double-check that my son, your fiancé, is resting." I turn to see Monica walk out of the room.

"I can't believe you are going to claim that my son is

your baby's father. You're a whore and probably have been sleeping with several other guys."

"No." I shake my head as tears roll down my face. This can't be happening. "He told me he'd make everything right if it happened. It was a mistake. I'm not sleeping with anyone but him." The words spill from my lips in defense.

"You're right." She smiles again. "Have a seat, Scout." She waves to the chairs behind me, and I take a seat. I know I'll regret this for the rest of my life, but I still hear her out.

An hour later I'm sitting at the top of Hagelberger looking down into Fairbanks and wondering how I ended up here. Cheryl had drawn up a document that states I'll never tell anyone that I suspect Thad of being my baby's father. That I will never come after him for money, and that I will abort the baby as soon as possible. It said by accepting the check in my hand, I agreed to all the terms. She wrote me out a check for five thousand dollars to pay for my "pain and suffering." I look at the check in my hand and the copy of the paperwork. I had no choice when Monica came back into the room. She said Thad said to get rid of me. I can't even tell my mom, who would help me with everything about this situation. I'm locked in and I'm scared because I don't want to get rid of my baby. It doesn't deserve the hate from that woman. I think of my parents. Of what I thought Thad was like and of my life here. For just a moment, I think I should just end it all, but I can't do that either. I look at the check and fold it up, then I slip it into my wallet as I make a phone call.

I weave the bike along Goldstream Road, careful of the frost heaves. The memories of my past still flash through my mind. Tears roll down my face, causing me to have to pull over. I wipe the tears away and start up again.

That phone call to my aunt was the only thing I could think of doing. I know it hurt my dad and mom. I know they blamed themselves, and I don't know how I could ever fix it. I finally showed my mom the contract, and she had my uncle look it over. I was sixteen and not a legal adult. I never cashed that check, so I'm not going to get in trouble. It took everything in us to hold my mom back. She still wants to kick Cheryl's ass.

I turn up Ballaine Road and then into the pull-off that was our spot. The large Dodge pickup parked there doesn't stop me. A lot of hikers and people pull over here. I sit on the bike, straddling it. Trying to get the memories and pain to subside. I don't hurt physically as much as I do emotionally. My head is dropped, and the tears are flowing.

"Hey, you okay?" I hear his deep voice and can't believe my luck. I look up and there he stands. The Dodge pickup must be his.

"What are you doing here?" I ask without thinking. He doesn't know it's me, but when he hears my voice he knows instantly.

"Scout?"

I nod and kick my stand down, then I swing my leg over and stand on the opposite side of him with my bike between us. I don't take off my helmet until I have my back to him. I slip off my gloves and wipe my face, praying it doesn't look like I was crying. I obviously failed when I turn around and he steps back. He moves around the bike faster than I thought a man his size could move.

"Are you okay? Are you hurting? You shouldn't be riding so soon after the attack." He brushes his hands into my short hair and pulls it back from my face.

"It's not that." I look up at him as he holds me so close. His hands cupping my head gently. He's so big, but he's always treated me with tenderness. That thought brings more tears because I couldn't even keep up my end of the bargain he wanted me to. "I'm sorry."

"We'll fix everything. It's okay, Sunshine."

I don't understand why he's kissing me. Why he's calling me that when he wanted me to have an abortion.

He leans down and gently kisses me. I can't stop my body's reaction. He's always pushed my buttons. He turns my head and deepens the kiss. Before I know it, my back is pressed against the side of his truck and he's pulling my legs around his hips. I wrap around him as I start to move against his erection through his jeans.

"Fuck, Sunshine, we need to stop, or I'm going to fuck you against my truck for everyone driving by to see." He groans when he pulls away. I lean forward and lick along his throat, slightly biting his neck.

"I want you." I tell him the same words he said to me weeks ago.

"We need to talk first." He doesn't release me but continues to stare at me with so many emotions on his face.

"I didn't hold up my end of the bargain. I've spoken to my attorney. He's getting everything written up. I don't want anything from you. If you don't want to help, that's okay. I make enough money to support us. And, I've done it without using any of that money.

He pushes back so fast I fall to the ground. My hand shoots out in time to catch myself from falling on my face. I stand up and take him in. His face is red, his lips tight, his jaw flexing.

"What the fuck?" he yells, and ducks in the water take off around us.

"I'm sorry I didn't follow the agreement. My attorney says I was under eighteen, so it wasn't legal."

"What the fuck are you talking about? What agreement?" He advances on me, and I slip to the side fast so he can't pin me to his truck again. I unzip my jacket and pull out my wallet. I pull out the check I've carried for years and throw it at him. We both watch as it flutters to the ground. When he bends down to pick it up, I'm in motion. I run for my bike and jump on it. He's holding the paper in his hand and slowly unfolding it. When he looks up at me, I don't know what I see in his face, but I know I have to get out of here.

"My attorney will be in touch," I scream as I snap my face shield in place and take off. I head back to my apartment and hide out.

Thad

I unfold the paper. It's an old check that hasn't been cashed. The date is the day I left for MEPS. I got called in early and had tried to call Scout, but her phone kept going to voicemail. I had asked my mother to go out there and tell her, but she told me in no uncertain terms she wouldn't and that there were rumors Scout had been seen in town with a young soldier.

I'm still processing everything, but all I can see is my mom's face the first time I saw her when I graduated from boot camp. She wouldn't look me in the eye and avoided all my questions about Scout. When I contacted her parents, they would only say she moved out of state.

I look at the check again. Five thousand dollars. It was signed by my mom. I look at the memo line and stop.

To take care of the little problem, and for pain and suffering.

The words roll through my head. I move to my truck as if in a trance. I head right for my parents' house. Ryder is in summer camp, so I don't have to worry about him. When I pull up, my mother is already on the front porch as a man carrying a clipboard moves away from her. He stops and looks at me before looking down at something on his board.

"You Thaddeus Abbott?" he asks me with surprise on his face. "Dang, two in one stop."

"Yes," I say and wait. He pulls something from under the top paper and hands me the official envelope.

"You've been served." He chuckles as he moves to his car.

I look at the envelope and up at my mother, who has one similar. Mine's thicker. I don't open it because I'm pretty sure I know what it is. I move toward my mother. She's opening her envelope.

"That little lying whore. Can't trust anyone these days."

I hear the words coming from her mouth and reach for the paper. I yank it from her hand. I quickly scan it, noting a cancellation of contract along with notes stating they will be seeking reparations for threats, defamation of character, and legal proceedings for unlawful contract.

I read the citation and can't believe the words. They swim across my vision for a moment. My eyes mist and I'm afraid I'm going to lose it. My own mother did this to the girl I loved.

"You fucking pressured an emotionally pregnant woman into signing a document, or you'd sue her, take away everything her parents worked for?" I yell at my mother so loud I know the neighbors and valley probably heard me. "You fucking paid to have my baby murdered? Your grandbaby? Is this fucking for real?" I shake the paperwork in her face. "How could you?"

"I was protecting you. She's a little tramp."

I lean over my mother, my body shaking. "If you weren't a fucking woman, I'd knock you out. I'm done. My attorney will be in contact with you also for loss of time with my daughter. You'd better hope Scout forgives me and I get to see Skyler, or I'll sue you for everything." I stomp back to my truck.

"She didn't abort the baby?" Her words make me pause.

I hold up the tattered check and wave it at her.

"No, she didn't. She didn't cash your fucking check either." I see the wheels turning behind her eyes.

"She broke the NDA." Her sinister smile has me stomping back toward her.

"No, she didn't. She was a minor. You're fucking out of plays. Give up."

My father pulls up and gets out of his vehicle. He takes one look at me and then my mother.

"What did you do, Cheryl?" His voice is laced with anger when he looks at her. I remain standing there and wait for her to admit what she did.

"I didn't do anything."

I wave my father over and show him the check. He looks at it, then at her.

"Oh, and there's this." I realize I still have the court paperwork in my hand. He takes it and then looks at me.

"Got a spare room I can use?"

"Yeah, I do."

He moves toward the stairs where my mother is still standing. He hands her the court document and then moves back to his car.

"Terrence, where are you going?" She moves, her voice quivering now. But I know it's fake, she's just playing him. She's the only person who calls my father by his full name. Everyone else calls him Terry.

"My attorney will be in contact. Pack your things, you are out of my house." He doesn't say more but gets back into his car and follows me out toward my place.

I can't believe she did this. When I get home, I dial Scout, but the phone goes directly to voicemail. I open the packet of papers I was served with and immediately shake my head.

Paternity testing, if I want it, and a visitation schedule.

She's not asking for money. She's giving me a choice. She thinks I wanted this. I don't know who I could talk to.

My phone rings and I hope it's Scout, but I see my sister's name on the display.

"Can I come see you?" Stormy asks. Her voice is so soft, but I can hear the tears in it.

"Yes." Even my voice is scratchy.

There's a knock on the door before I even hang up, and I know she was sitting at the end of my driveway just waiting.

"Why is Dad's car here?" she asks when I open the door.

He moves from the kitchen where he was giving Ryder a snack to hold him over until I go pick up dinner.

"How about I go get the pizza with Ryder and you two have your talk," Dad offers, and I nod at him. He moves to my sister and without question pulls her into his arms. "I've missed you so much, baby girl," he says against the top of her head. She holds him tight, and I smile. Watching my father and sister make up is the best thing to come out of today. I know it's going to take more time, but they needed this. "Be here when I get back. I want to talk to you." He chucks her chin, and she smiles.

"Okay, Daddy." Her voice cracks, and Ryder comes over to hug her.

After they leave, I sit down at the table with her.

"Scout came and talked to me today. I know everything."

"You do?"

"Well, I knew part of it. Now I got the parts I didn't overhear." She chuckles softly. "Mother talked loudly, and Monica couldn't keep a secret for the life of her. They played Scout." She takes a drink of the water I sat in front of her. "Scout didn't know you were gone already. They acted like you were in your room. I didn't know that part until she told me. But you need to know she thought you broke up with her and left her pregnant. Monica had a ring and everything."

I pause and it hits me. "Did you see the ring?" I demand. She doesn't lean back in fear of me. She knows I'm not mad at her, just the situation.

"No, but I remember seeing mother with it after the fact. She used to store it in her desk. Why?"

"Because I bought a ring for Scout. She said she wasn't ready to get married at the time. Said she still had a year of school, and I could change my mind. But that she was still and would always be mine."

Stormy looks to the side as she bites her lip. She reaches for her large slouch bag and pulls it onto her lap. I watch as she digs around in it for a bit before she pulls out a key.

"Okay, I lied. Here is the key to a safety deposit box. The ring along with some other information from that day are in it. I stole the ring right afterward.

Mother did hide it in the desk. It's how I've kept her off my back all these years."

I shake my head, my eyebrows raising to the roof. My eyes grow big. "You blackmailed our mother? You were only thirteen when this happened."

"Yeah, well, I didn't do the blackmail until later. I just knew that Scout needed help. She looked so scared. Scout doesn't know about this."

"She won't hear it from me. You need to tell her."

"I will. I knew our mother and Monica were wrong. I knew they were playing Scout. I also knew Sky was yours the first time I saw her." She chuckles, and we continue talking for a bit. I'm still worked up and move to the porch when my dad and Ryder come home. I dial Scout's number, and again it goes directly to voicemail.

"Scout, Sunshine. Please call me back. I'm not mad. You were played. We both were, and I'm stupid for not questioning my mother all these years. Please. I know Skyler is my daughter. I don't need a paternity test. I now know why you stayed with that idiot who beat you. You thought that's all you deserved after what I did to you. I want to try to work this out. If not, at least I want to be a part of my daughter's life."

I hang up and go back into the house knowing I'm going to have to fight Scout on this. She's not going to roll over and let me walk back into her life. Maybe she'll let me in Skyler's life but not hers. She might be right. I might not deserve her anymore.

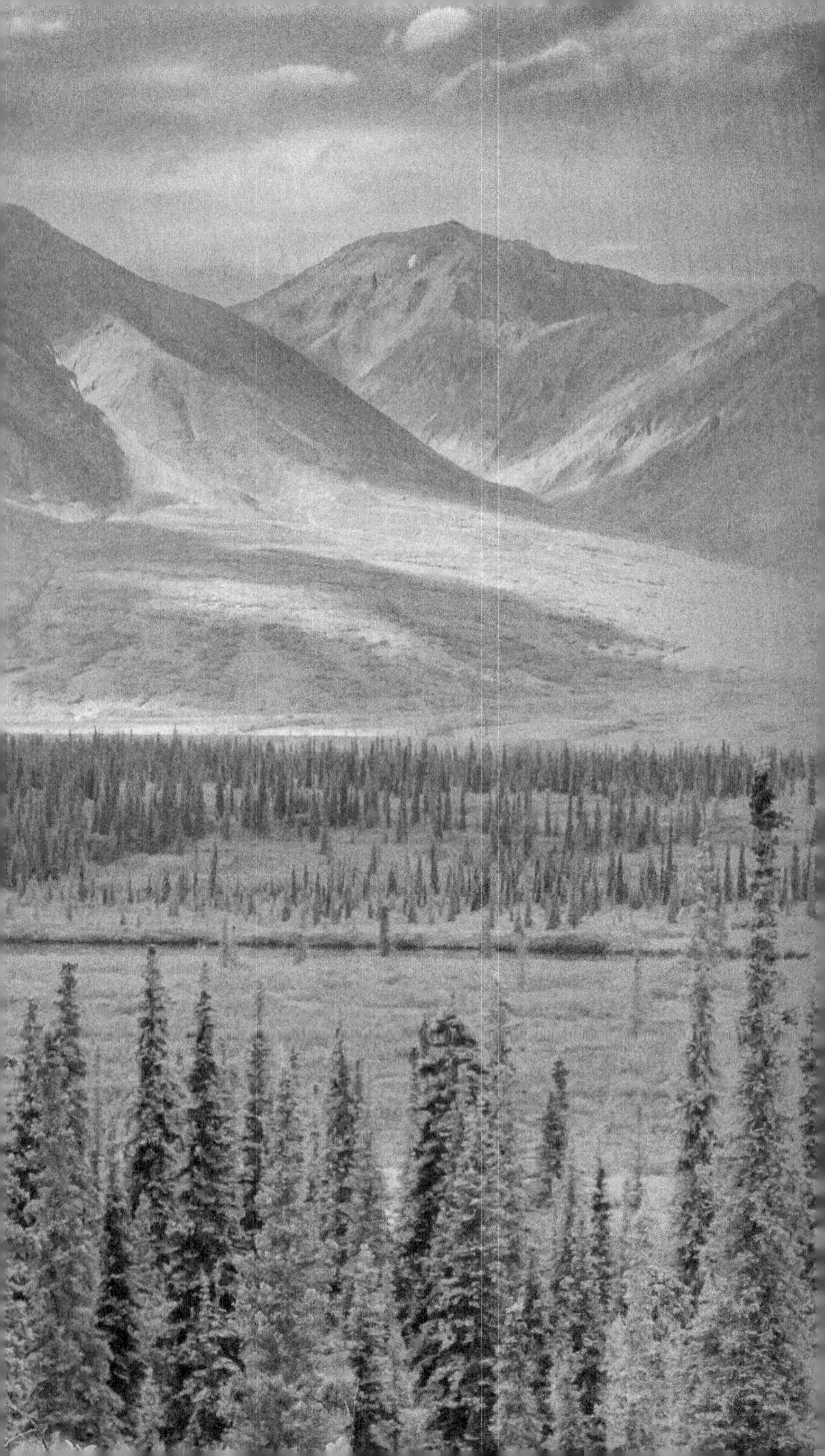

NINE
SCOUT

I've been a chickenshit. I'm avoiding him, and I hide out in my offices when someone pulls in. I stay at home on the weekends unless we have a run. If Stormy needs something, I have her contact River. I'm not willing to discuss it. I know he got the papers. He's been in contact with Joel, but he won't sign the visitation paperwork until I meet with him.

What if he's pissed?

Stormy told me Thad wasn't there at all that day. That he'd already left for MEPS but couldn't reach me. I remember my phone breaking and having to use my mom's. I called my aunt from it. Could everything have been a huge mistake?

There has been too much against us. I can't let it all go. The hurt is the worst. I wanted Thad to be my one, but he wasn't. He was right when he said I stayed with Phantom because I thought that's what I deserved. I'd been beat down already.

The phone rings from the coffee table as I watch *Ferdinand* with Sky. We went to the movie theater when it came out, and since I bought it for her on digital, she watches it several times. I have to say I'm getting a bit sick of it, but at least she hasn't watched it as much as she did *Frozen*. I'm ready for her to move on to a different movie though. Skyler and I had a talk finally about her father. I've never told her that he was dead or that he didn't want her, even though I thought that. Instead, I told her he was busy in the military and someday she would meet him. So now I've told her he's here and wants to meet her if she wants to meet him.

"Yeah." I answer the phone while watching Sky dance around laughing at the movie.

"We need you down here right now. The bitch is back and causing issues with your staff," River says into the phone. She and a few of the other girls were going to go to the bar and hang out.

I look down at my outfit I changed into after I showered from work. I'm in a crop top corset over another black crop top and shorts. The tops are so tight my breasts are pushed up. I guess part of me wanted to go hang out with them, but I was scared someone would know I was having doubts. Doubts about him.

"Frenchie is on her way to watch Little Bear." River knows me so well.

I stand and move back to the table where I set my platform Goth open-toe heels. I slip them on and buckle them. I'm standing up and fluffy my hair in the mirror and checking my makeup I put on earlier when Frenchie hits the top stair.

"I knew it. So did Jinx. You're up here hiding. Go down there and tell that B off." Frenchie laughs and moves to sit down on the sofa. She won't cuss in front of Sky. Frenchie was training to be a governess or nanny before she joined us, so she loves that she has Skyler to watch and keep an eye on. I pay her well to be there for her, but I don't expect her to when I'm not working. She's practically family, as far as I'm concerned.

"But you wanted to go out tonight." I try really hard to get out of this. If troopers are called again, will he show up?

"Go, now," she orders me and points.

"Bye, Sky, baby." I kiss my daughter and then move down the stairs. I watch her dancing around with Rufus. I know between Frenchie and him my baby girl is always safe.

When I enter the back hallway, I can hear voices over the music from the bar. I push open my office door and check out the cameras. I see Monica sitting at a table with her friends again. Stormy is serving them. One of the girls has a crown and sash on. She's obviously the bride-to-be from the amount of penis necklaces around her neck. They all take a shot, and I watch as Monica scolds Stormy and demands something. Stormy moves away toward the bar, and I look at the bar camera as she puts in another order. I check the POS system and see that another round is being comped for a different shot. A top-shelf liquor.

I've had enough. I head out into the main area, avoiding the bar and going straight to their table. One of the girls watches me approach and whispers something to Monica. She knows I'm coming, so I'm not unprepared for the words that come out of her mouth.

"Oh, Holly, I can't wait until we are all sitting here celebrating my bachelorette party now that Thad has proposed to me." She laughs and it's so fake. There was a video circulating on social media of the two of them at Cookie Jar. It looks innocent, but she's been bombarding the feeds with comments that they are back together and going to be setting a date soon. I doubt it because of the messages he's sending me.

"That's funny because I think he just told me about an hour ago that his focus right now is his daughter." I let the words out, knowing this is the first time I've acknowledged he's Sky's father.

"Excuse me." She spins around so fast I watch her eyes bounce for a moment while she gets her bearings. "What daughter?"

"Our daughter."

Now she's up and out of the chair. She and I are about the same height in these shoes. I look her in the eye and tip my head to the side.

"You don't have a baby with him," she hisses quietly because she's under the assumption that the NDA is still in place. Little does she know. That means that she hasn't been served yet, which is surprising. I know Uncle Joel was finding more evidence against her, so maybe that's the delay.

"I do. She's nine. Has his eyes too," I say loud enough that the girls at the table hear me. A pin could drop in the building and everyone would hear it.

"You violated the agreement," she hisses again.

I lean ever so tiny bit toward her. "Are you saying you know about a secret document that I was forced to sign along with hush money given to me? Trying to force me to have an abortion when I was only sixteen." People gasp around us, and the music is absent so just about everyone can hear me now.

I watch as she steps back and looks around in shock. She recovers pretty quickly as the fake smile is back on her fake as fuck lips. "I don't know what you're talking about. I wouldn't be party to having a minor's rights violated." She tries to flip her hair, but it doesn't go far as it's pulled back in a ponytail.

I laugh and it sounds so wrong. I know it, and my girls move closer. I'm sure they have a feeling what's about to happen. I need this. I need to beat the shit out of someone or fuck someone's brains out. Since my body only wants Thad, I guess I'm going to have to fuck up his wannabe girlfriend.

"Oh, sweetheart, you were not only a part of it, you were a witness. I have the paperwork in a safe place. I used to have the five-thousand-dollar check in my wallet, but Thad has that now." She steps back, shocked. Again, I lean forward wanting to further piss her off. "He knows everything. But don't worry, you'll soon be served papers, just like I had his mother served."

"For what?" she sputters.

I step toward her. I need her to strike me first for this to work.

"For defamation of character and forcing me to sign that nondisclosure agreement." My grin is big but doesn't reach my eyes. One of the girls at the table is an idiot.

"Can you really do that?" she asks.

I turn to look at her, and it's the opening Monica needed. But I've got excellent peripheral vision and I'm ready for the slap. It cracks through the quiet of the bar, and I swing around. I punch her hard in the face. Her nose buckles under the blow, and blood flies through the air, some of it hitting me. The copper smell only ignites my anger more. I've wanted this for years.

I laugh and she comes at me, but I'm ready for her. I have her spun around with her arm up her back again.

"This feels really familiar. You must like when your bitches here give it to you in the ass with that vibrating dildo."

One of the girls jumps up, but Rivet takes care of her. She has her spun around and pushes her out the door. Every one of my girls grabs a girl and drags them out kicking and screaming. I have the ringleader, and when I get to the deck, I push her away and kick her. She goes sprawling to the ground, face-planting. It's not enough. I want to step off the porch and beat her some more, but the parking lot is full of red and blue lights.

"Don't ever come back. You are banned from these premises. And don't ever fuck with the Devil's Handmaidens." The girls all look at us, but it's Monica who stands up and starts to come at me again. "Are you sure you want to try this again, because I'll do more than bust your nose?" I threaten her.

"I'm calling the police," she yells. "You assaulted me."

"Nope." I pop the p. "I have a room full of patrons who will swear under oath that you smacked me first. Oh yeah, I have the mark too." I wave my hand down my face in a Vanna White imitation.

"I'll get you."

"That sounds like a threat," the trooper says from behind her, and she jumps. "Ms. Granger, looks like you're going back to jail. I think the last time your father said if this happened again you were going to have to serve the whole time, he wasn't bailing you out."

We all laugh, but mine dies when I see him leaning against his pickup. He nods to the other officers before he moves toward us. I watch as Monica stops him, begging him to save her. I turn and head back into the bar. I don't want to see them together. I can't stomach that tonight. I don't stop until I reach my office.

The shot glass and bottle are waiting for me.

Stormy knew I'd need it. I pour a glass and think twice before I take the bottle and drink directly from it. This is what he's got me resorting to. I'm going to have to drink until I pass out to get any sleep. The door closes and I hear a click as I swing around. The bottle is still in my hand. He takes it from me and takes a swig himself.

"I've been trying to reach you." His voice is deep and husky. I squirm because it's a direct link to my clit. It's always been that way. His eyes move up and down my body.

"I know." My voice sounds all breathy and wrong. I shake my head and try again. "I needed time."

"Have you had enough time?" He pushes his body into mine, pressing me into the desk. I look up at him and bite my lip.

Thad

My sister told me to come out. She said Monica was here causing trouble. She said Scout was avoiding the bar but would help if they called her. I know it was a setup. Well, except for the Monica part. Scout's crew decided she was done moping. I'm glad they took pity on me, but as I stand over her watching that pink tongue glide against her lips before she bites the full bottom one, I don't want to talk about Skyler. I want to fuck her instead.

That thought only coalesces in my brain for a moment and my mouth is on hers. I nip her lip and she opens for me. When her tongue slides against mine, I notice the difference immediately. She's not fighting for dominance, she's giving in to me. She wants this too.

I completely dominate her mouth, and when I finally pull away, we are both breathless. I lift her up and nibble on her neck.

"I'm going to fuck you right here, Scout. You hear me?" I growl against her ear.

"Yes." She sighs, and I pick her up again. I hold her in one arm against my chest while the other undoes her shorts. I push her against the door and yank them and her thong down over her heels. I'm not going to be able to strip her bare in this office. Her skin is covered in tattoos. I unbuckle my belt and push my jeans down. I rub my hard as fuck cock through her drenched folds before I slam up into her. She cries out and I hold her face in my hand.

"Don't you dare let any other men hear your sex cries. I'll have to shoot them, and they don't allow conjugal visits at FCC." She nods and bites her lip. Her hands go into my hair and pull. But she doesn't quiet. I'm going to be in Fairbanks Correctional Center before the night is out if this keeps up.

I move slowly, trying to get her body to accommodate to me again. She's still tight as fuck, and I'm over the moon with the fact that she hasn't been with very many men. She tugs my head back from watching where we are connected.

I look her in the eye as she leans forward. Right before she kisses me, she hisses, "You promised me you were going to fuck me. Now get to it before I sit you down and ride this cock." I almost nut right there with those words.

"My Sunshine likes it rough?" I bite her lip and pull. She moans, and I feel more of her leaking out around my cock. I pull out and flip her around to face the door. She braces her hands against it. I want to be gentle as she's still recovering from her attack, but I can't seem to. I need to prove she's real and not a damn dream. With a grip on her hips, I slam back in and we both groan. "Fuck, this office better be soundproof."

"It is." She moans loudly.

"I've missed this tight little pussy," I say, and she moans again. She used to blush when I'd talk dirty, but she loved it. Now we are both older and I'm going to tell her everything I plan to do. "I'm going to come so deep in this fucking pussy everyone will know who you belong to when they see my cum leaking from you."

She cries out and comes. I smack her ass hard. "I didn't say you could come, Sunshine. Now you're going to get it." I pull out and pick her up. I move across the room and clear the desk with an arm. Glass falls to the floor. Whiskey splashes on my boots. I drop her onto the now cleared desk. "I'm going to get a taste and build you up again. Don't you come until I tell you to. You hear me, Sunshine."

"Yes, Thad," she says, and I drop to my knees, opening up her folds.

I take in her pink folds that are darker from me slamming into her. Her cum leaking from her body. I blow along her clit, and she moans as she arches and moves around on the desk. When I lean forward and take her clit deep into my mouth, she cries out and screams. I push her back to the desk. I eat her out like the starved man I am for her. I've missed her taste. I've missed so much. But I'm not going to keep thinking about that. I've got her now and she's mine again. I'll fight tooth and nail to prove that. I'm never letting her go this time.

"Thad, please," she begs as I push two fingers into her. I pump them in and out of her and can't take any more. Jealous of my fingers, I need my cock in her again. I stand up and slowly slide into her. I watch as her body stretches to accommodate my wide girth. "Yes." Her head is trashing around now.

I hold her hip in one and slide the other up her body, yanking her top up so I can get to those breasts. I hear the material ripping, but I don't care and force it where I want it. Leaning forward, I take her nipple in my mouth while I pluck the other one. When I pull away, she's looking at me. Focused on me.

"Thad," she begs. I know she's holding it back. I

can feel the flutters of her vaginal muscles around my cock.

"Are you on birth control?" I ask the important question.

"Yes." She moans. I hate the answer, but I'll get her to wanting to carry my next baby.

I grab her hips, thrusting in hard and pulling her onto me harder. The heavy desk starts moving from the force of my body.

"Come for me," I order her, and she screams my name as I bury myself deep inside her. I feel like I'm being turned inside out as I come hard. My knees buckle and I fall over her body, caging her in with my arms.

"This right here changes everything, Sunshine." I watch the emotions play across her face. I flex my hips so she gets what I'm saying.

"It can't. You're the law and I'm not." She starts closing herself off to me, but I hold her chin and look deep into her eyes.

"We'll make it work. I know you don't purposely break the law. I know what you do. I'm going to make this right, if it's the last thing I do." I give her everything in my heart so she can see it. She gives me the slightest nod.

When I slip from her body, I watch as my cum slides out of her.

"One day I'm going to get you pregnant again." I can't tell her I love her yet because she isn't ready for that. But I'll give her this to ponder.

"I don't know if I want to do that again." She slips from the desk and grabs some tissue to wipe herself up. She adjusts her tops, but I can see that they are ripped down the side.

"Take my shirt." I offer her the flannel I'm wearing over a T-shirt.

She throws her other shirts in the trash and takes the flannel. She partially buttons it before tying it so you still see her belly with the twinkle of jewelry.

"We need to keep this from Skyler until she gets used to who you really are. I also don't want my club to know yet. I talked to Skyler already, but she doesn't know you're her father. Just that he's here and wants to see her."

"I'm pretty sure they know we are fucking again."

"Well, they can think that but nothing else."

"Why?"

"Because you are a trooper and used to be public enemy number one with them." She laughs at the last part, and I'm glad she had them to support and help her. "I'm their president. They need to know I'll do anything for them, even break the law."

"How long have they known I'm Sky's father?"

She turns to look at me as she slips her thong and shorts back on. "They just found that part out. Only River knew the truth and then my aunt. I told my mom a few weeks ago, but she said she's known all along. My father knew. I told him a few weeks before he was killed." Her words hurt because my mother caused this riff between her and her family. "By the way, you might want to keep your mother away from mine. Mine wants to kick her ass."

"Good. My father is having her removed from the house. They are getting a divorce."

"What?" Her eyes flare wide in shock, and I pull her into my body.

"Sunshine, she lied and manipulated you. My father doesn't put up with that. You and I both know that."

"But divorce?"

"It's something that was going to happen for a while now. It was just a matter of time before she fucked up enough that my father couldn't look past it. The fact he lost nine years with his granddaughter is more than he wants to think about."

"I still don't like it." Her voice is soft. I tip her chin up, holding her firmly so she doesn't doubt what I'm going to say.

"My mother made her bed years ago. It's time she laid in it and faced the consequences of her actions." I kiss her forehead, then I softly kiss her lips. She falls into the kiss for a moment before she stiffens and pulls away.

"We can't do sweet and cuddly. A fuck here and there is okay. But no being sweet." I know why she's keeping this wall up, but I still hate it.

"Tomorrow is Ryder's birthday party. Are you still bringing Sky?"

"My mother and aunt planned to. But I think we should wait before she finds out who you are. I don't want to ruin Ryder's day." Something settles deep in my soul that she cares for my son this much, but I'm not going to let her deny my family any longer. "No. You come and we can tell her after the party."

"Fine."

There is a knock on the door. Scout opens it, and I see my sister standing there with a knowing grin.

Scout starts doing her job as owner and president of her club. I sit in the corner of the bar, nursing a coke and praying she'll let me stay the night with her. I can't wait to get back into her body. I'm obsessed with it already.

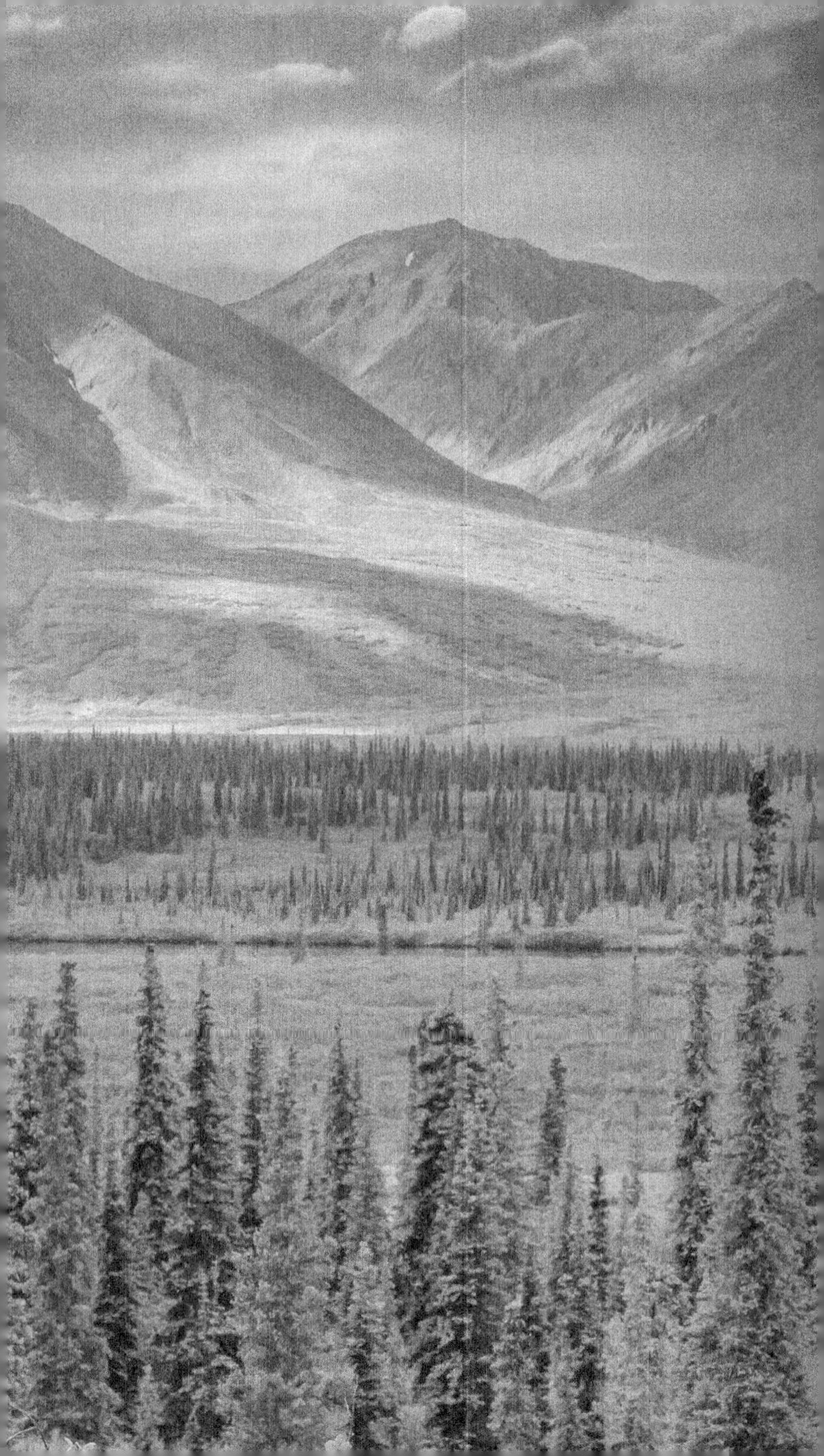

TEN
SCOUT

The wind hits my face and I sigh. This weekend was just what I needed. A small respite from the emotions at home. I think over the week before. It was like she knew. The moment we pulled into Thad's driveway off Goldstream, Skyler piped up from the back seat.

"Ryder's dad is my dad, isn't he?" Her question is soft, but it reminds me how smart she is. How in tune with others she is.

"Yeah, baby. He is." I won't lie to her.

The party went off without a hitch, unless you count all the married and single women who were trying to get Thad's attention. But he was focused on Skyler and Ryder.

I then went to work and only texted him. Told him I had plans, then I tried to adjust to my body wanting him again. I want him all the time. I wake from dreams of him and what he did to me in my office.

River and I talked about it, but I'm still not sure where he fits into my life except to be there for Skyler.

That's why this weekend was so important. River, Skyler, Minuet, my mom, and I all came down to Denali for the weekend. Just the girls. Mom is driving my truck, while River, Minuet, and I are on our bikes. I hold out two fingers as some bikes head south opposite of us. They do the same two-finger wave and I'm excited. We need to make a run down here as a club.

My aunt was supposed to come with us, but she cancelled at the last minute. I have a feeling I know what's going on with her. From the moment she met Thad's dad, Terry, they've been talking, texting, and more. I warned her he was on the rebound, and she told me to mind my own business. The other girls stayed back to give us some time together. I left Rivet in charge.

We are coming up on Nenana, and I promised Sky we could stop at the Monderosa Bar and have a burger. My mom was telling her how good they were. She had pizza at Prospectors in Denali. Cinnamon Rolls at a local café. Ice Cream at Miller's. The girl probably gained enough weight for her next growth spurt this weekend alone. My mother and I laughed at her as she ran up and down the boardwalks and asked to buy touristy things.

The smile on my face is huge when we pull into the parking lot of Monderosa. My cell rings in my pocket, and I pull it out. Seeing it's my aunt, I decide to tease her.

"Decided you were wrong and having second thoughts now?" I chuckle as I wait for my mom to pull in behind us.

"Scout, you need to come home, now." Her voice is tight. I freeze, worried she's going to tell me someone else has died.

"Who?" I ask, and River is by my side, holding my arm as I shake. I see Thad in my mind. One of the girls. My uncle. Everyone I'm worried about because they still can't figure out why my father was killed and who did it. Thad is working a new angle and it has something to do with a truck he found burned up a couple of weeks ago.

"Your parents' place." The words don't register.

"What?" I shake my head, confused. River takes the phone from me.

"Vixen, what's going on." I hear her ask as my mom and Sky move toward us. "Fuck. We're on our way, but we can't speed too much." She twirls her hand in the air, indicating for everyone to load back up. Sky starts to get upset, but my mom knows something is up and gets her in the truck before they pull out. River looks at me after she hangs up. "We need to beat your mom there. Her house was vandalized and part of it burned."

"Rufus?" I ask because he stayed there with Vixen while we came on this trip. The hotel wouldn't allow dogs.

"Vixen picked him up earlier and took him back to the clubhouse."

I nod and start up my Indian Scout and take off, passing my mom in the truck. The girls stay with me, and we make the ninety-minute drive in under sixty. We took most of the side roads and only sped a little bit. I pull up at my parents' place and hold the tears back. Only part of the house was destroyed, but it's still a total loss. Thad is standing there in his uniform with my aunt next to him. Another man in a station uniform is beside them. I expect he's the fire investigator.

My truck comes to a stop, and I hear the door. I turn as I watch my mom fall to her knees. My father built this house for her as a wedding gift. They lived there together until the day he died. To lose it and him could be too much. I rush to her, and my aunt is there with me. We hold her up as River approaches Thad and the investigator.

I can tell just from looking at him that Thad is upset about something. I look at my aunt, and she nods.

"Momma, I'll be right back." I disengage her arms from around me. Looking into my truck, I see Skyler crying. First, I need to take care of her. I open the door and settle her, letting her know that Rufus wasn't here. She sits in the seat and nods. "I need to go talk to Thad."

"Can I come?" she asks softly, and I turn to look at him. He shakes his head ever so slightly. It's bad and he doesn't want her near it.

"Stay with me, Little Bear," Frenchie says as she takes her in her arms.

"Thank you."

As I walk toward Thad, part of me wants to run to him and jump in his arms. I want the comfort I know he'll give me, but I can't do that.

"What's up?" I try to hold the quiver out of my voice.

"Hello, Ms. Keller. I'm Thompson, an investigator with the North Star Borough. From my preliminary investigation, I've determined an accelerate was used. It was arson. Trooper Abbott is investigating the possible murder." He moves away to go through more debris, and I turn to Thad with panicked eyes.

"Someone died?"

He steps closer to me. "We don't know as of yet. We haven't found a body, but there is lots of blood. Crime scene should be here shortly to confirm if it's animal or human."

"Okay." I hear the quiver in my voice.

"There was a message, for you and your mother." His voice is husky and full of emotion.

"Where?"

"Follow me. Be careful." He directs River and me through the debris field and up the porch stairs to the front door. When he opens it, I see the damage to all the furniture. Things are torn up and trashed. And there's so much blood. But it's the message on the wall written in blood that stops me.

> *Lucky you weren't here to meet me. Your husband didn't survive, and you were supposed to be next on my list. I'll get you soon, don't worry. Riddler, you can hide her away, but she will die and so will your bastard before I'm done. I will have my revenge.*

My blood runs cold. This is all about me. I turn and stomp out of the house. My aunt must have seen the message already. I pull out my cell and bark orders into it.

"Load up, now," I growl at my mother. "Two front two rear. We'll be surrounded shortly." I direct the other girls.

My mom goes to argue with me. "Scout, I need to see."

"Mom, get in the truck, now. If you can't drive, I will, but you will go to my house and stay with me until further notice."

I turn to River. I'm not Scout, the daughter or friend now. I'm Riddler, and I'll win this game if I have to die trying.

"Jinx, I want Scarlett's location. See if there are any nomads who would like to come help us out."

"On it, Prez," Jinx responds without question.

"Scout." His voice breaks through everything, but I'm not going to follow the rules to protect my family.

"No." I turn toward him. "I need Rufus back before the night is out. He'll protect Little Bear."

Thad moves right up to me, pressing his big body into mine. "I'll get a protection detail on you all."

I shake my head and look up at him. "You can't protect them the way I can."

Because Denali is a national park, I couldn't have my gun on me. But as soon as I get on my property, I'll be armed at all times. For now, I walk back to my truck and lift the small seat on the back passenger side. I open the safe that holds a spare there.

"This isn't how you do it." Thad tries to stop me, but I slip the small .38 into the chest pocket of my leather jacket.

"This is how I handle it. This is why you and I can't work. Besides, do you want whoever that is"—I wave my hand toward the house—"to focus on you or Ryder?" I swing a leg over my bike, and we head out.

Jinx and I lead with Frenchie and Vixen bringing up the tail. Before we are even back on the main highway, I hear the other bikes coming. They surround the truck too.

Thad

The drive out to Ptarmigan Falls takes longer than I want in the late afternoon traffic through the city. I sometimes hate that the trooper post is right in the city, but I took the quickest way out of town via the Johansen Expressway. Dylan sits quietly next to me. He's been here since Tuesday, and so far, we've gotten a lot of information we didn't have before. The links between several cases are all tied together, and my girl is right in the center of it.

I watched her pull away on Sunday and knew in my gut she wasn't going to stop. That I might not ever get her back. I thought about what she said about me being the law and her not. That's ridiculous because I know she won't step over that line unless she has to. But now with our daughter and her mother being threatened and that person saying they killed her father, I know she will step over that line. I've spent hours this last week wondering if I'd do it too. I won't know until the situation comes up, but that's my daughter who was threatened. My woman and my daughter.

I knew I needed to find out what I could do to get some help. Law-abiding help that would also not think twice about protecting my family. I called Dylan, and he came running. We're pretty sure now that her attack and her father's murder are connected. We have evidence that her father's murder is also connected to the murder of a young runaway.

I haven't seen Scout or Skyler since Sunday at her

mother's place. It's now Friday and I'm jonesing to see them both. My body aches to hold them both. At night when I kiss Ryder goodnight, I think about kissing Sky too. I think about climbing into bed with Scout and having my family all together.

I'd called Scout earlier in the week, but she didn't return my call. She texted, saying she'd call me when she could. I knew it was a way to avoid me. She thinks she's protecting Ryder and me by keeping her distance.

"This place has built up a lot over the years," Dylan says as we drop into Ptarmigan Falls.

"Yeah. Even in the two months since Scout came home. She's done a lot. Her restoration business brings a lot of traffic this way," I say, distracted as I watch a motorcycle coming down behind us.

I pull into the parking lot between the two businesses and through the gate that is open during business hours. It will be closing soon as I waited until the end of the day to come out here. I don't see the motorcycle behind me any longer. I grab my hat as I exit my vehicle. We are here on official business, so both Dylan and I are in uniform.

His lieutenant didn't make him take time off to come up and help me with this case because of the interconnection of cases. But Dylan would have taken the time off if he needed to. That's how close of friends we are.

We step out and move toward the nearest bay, and Scout walks out. She's not in her coveralls. Instead, she's in tight leather pants and a blue slinky silky tank top under her cut. Her friend Rivet is standing there watching. She is also dressed similarly in sexy over-the-top leather.

"Sorry, we are closed." Scout laughs and looks past us to the SUV. "Plus, I don't see anything I can restore on your rig except maybe the logo." Others laugh around us.

Several women move from the clubhouse toward us. I don't recognize a couple of them. A shorter woman with dyed red hair and piercing eyes watches us approach. But the girl with black and white hair is the one I'm looking for.

"We're here to speak to Avery Nickles and you." I point to Scout.

"You can talk with all of us around. We have very few secrets," Scout says, and I notice River moving out of the office to stand back with them. She too is dressed up instead of in her normal work attire.

"Are you sure?" I look directly at Avery when she steps into my line of sight, and she nods.

"I'm sorry to say we found a lot of blood in the back of a burned-out pickup. It's taken a couple of weeks for the DNA results to come back to us, but it was your sister's." I pause, expecting her to start crying. What I don't expect is for her to dive at me. She is punching and hitting me. I hold her back, knowing her hostility is not aimed at me, per se. Scout grabs her and pushes her back. The short redhead grabs her while Ginger holds her back too.

"If you had taken my report seriously, she wouldn't be hurt." She pauses in her rant, and I see the moment she realizes what I said. "Did you find a body? Was it just blood? How much? Where?" Her tears start immediately, and her friends wrap her up in their arms.

"It was a significant amount. We couldn't find any more evidence regarding your sister other than that." I take a deep breath. "I'm sorry your concerns weren't taken seriously. But I assure you both Dylan and I are completely on this case." I wave my hand toward Dylan.

"Why did you need to talk to me too?" Scout asks, and I look down at her. I don't want to be here for this, but there is no stopping it now.

"We found a pair of nitrile gloves in the cab of the truck. They were turned inside out so the killer's DNA was destroyed in the fire. But since the outside was turned in, we were able to find traces of your father's DNA." I watch the emotions play over her face.

"And?" She stands firm, putting on a front with her people behind her. But I see the pain and hurt in her eyes.

"Scout, it was the truck that we saw on the security feeds. Your father's murder is connected to Avery's sister's death."

"She's dead? You said you didn't find a body."

I take another deep breath before I begin again. "We didn't find a body, but based on the amount of blood that was in the bed, it's very unlikely she survived. We are inspecting other parts of the truck now to see if we can tell where it's been other than here and where it was found."

"I also have reason to believe your attack in Palmer has a direct tie to these cases," Dylan says.

Scouts shakes her head and stops. "Okay," she says as she closes her eyes for a moment as she tries to shore up her emotions. I so want to pull her into my arms, but I can tell she won't let me.

"We recovered a stolen vehicle a few feet off the trail where you were found. There was no DNA, not even a hair, but your mother's address was found on a piece of paper," Dylan continues.

She holds up a hand. "Wait. Stop. Why would they make sure none of their DNA was left behind, but they left a piece of paper to be found?"

"We confirmed a report of another vehicle stolen from the entrance to Jim Creek, not far from where you were running. We're working the theory he took that after he attacked you and didn't go back to this car. The note was under the seat where he would've had to lean down to look for it." Dylan stops and changes course. "I asked you before if you had any enemies. We have not been able to confirm if Mr. Smith is still being detained."

"He isn't," a deep voice says from behind us, and we all look. I hear a couple of gasps, but I don't take my eyes off the intruder. Something tells me he's extremely dangerous. It's not all the tattoos, even on his face. It's not the gun and knife strapped to his belt. It's the way he carries himself.

"Reaper?" I turn as I see movement out of my peripheral. River walks up and smacks him full on the face. He doesn't stop her. "What the fuck are you doing here?" she yells at him.

He rubs his cheek and chuckles. "Guess I deserved that."

"You fucking think. You left me. You fucking left me in that room."

"Baby." He moves to grab her, and this time when she goes to hit him, he stops her. "We have a lot to talk about. I came for you. I had to take care of business, and then I came for you."

"Well, go to hell. I don't want you." She moves back to stand next to Scout.

"Officers…" He looks us up and down again. "Troopers, sorry. You'll find out that one Stanley "Phantom" Smith is no longer in the state of Kentucky custody. He was paroled several months ago."

"How do you know that?" I don't like this guy or trust him.

He squints and looks over our shoulders. "I can't tell you that." He pinches his lips.

"Yes, you fucking can. If Phantom is coming after Riddler, we need to know," River grits out as she moves toward him again.

"Baby, let me talk to these guys alone. You go inside and get me a beer." Her fist swings out again and she cracks him in the face faster than he thought. "Yep, deserved that too." He holds his jaw and looks at River again. "Keep it up, baby girl, and I'm going to fuck you against that wall to prove who owns you."

"Try it and I'll stick you with your Bowie," River bites out.

"Reaper, what are you doing here?" Scout asks.

"Can we talk?" He nods his head and works his jaw. "Damn, baby, your hit has gotten better." When he sees River squeezing her hand and working her fingers, he is at her side instantly. "Fucking A, baby girl." He takes her hand and presses into her. "You can't damage your fingers, you know that. I'm sorry." He leans down and kisses her forehead. She tries to pull away, but he keeps her close with an arm around her. "You can come too." He drags her around, and it's the first time since River and Scout moved back here that I actually see River off balance. She is completely off step with this guy around.

"Let's go to my office." Scout moves to the clubhouse, and we follow along. The main room is decorated, and I see a DJ setting up. "Excuse us, the girls wanted to have a party since there are a lot of bikers in town for the Golden Days festivities." She points around, and I note the number of men around here for it being an all women MC.

When we turn to the left and enter the second room, my gaze goes to the large desk. Images of me taking her on the desk in the bar run through my mind and I have to push them back before I embarrass myself. She moves to sit in the chair, and I watch as Reaper takes a seat and pulls River onto his lap. She tries to move, but he won't let her go.

I shake my head as I pull my hat off. "River, do I need to help you?" I offer, and the guy looks at me like he wants to kill me.

"Dude, I don't know you, but you don't want to come between—" River covers his mouth with her hand, stopping him from saying more. He mumbles behind it and gives her a look, his tattooed eyebrow rising high.

"I was asking River," I clarify, not afraid of him.

He starts to stand up, but she pushes him down, something I know she wouldn't be able to do if not for the fact he's afraid of hurting her.

"Thad, it's okay. I know how to handle Reaper myself." She raises her brow as he growls behind her hand.

"Okay, Reaper, what do you want to talk to us about? Why wasn't I notified? I should've been," Scout says.

Reaper pulls River's hand from his mouth and kisses her palm. The look the man has in his eyes for her is pure love, but she is giving him hate back.

"You should've been notified, but I don't think the authorities want to let you know they lost him a week after he went on parole. He up and disappeared. If you are having issues, I know it's him."

"He was supposed to serve a minimum of ten

years, even if he got good behavior, because of the aggression of his attack. He also attacked the officers who arrested him." Scout stands and starts pacing. It's my turn to console my girl, and I move toward her. She starts to put up a hand but stops and lets me pull her into my body. I turn with her, and we look back at Reaper.

"Well. Well. Well. Riddler found herself a man. It's about fucking time."

"Continue. How do you know he's out? How do you know all this?" I've had enough with this joker.

He takes a deep breath and looks at River before turning to look at Scout and me. "I'm former ATF. I was under for the last eight years. I can't show you a badge or anything, but…" He reaches into his pocket and pulls out his wallet. He opens it and pulls out a card. "He'll be able to verify who I am. My real name is Klay Ulrich." He sits back down and grabs River in his long arms. He tips her chin to look at him. "I'm here to get my woman back, to protect her from Phantom, and to warn you." He turns to Scout and nods before he turns back to River. "In that order, babe. I quit. Walked away because I'm not going to keep putting either of us in danger."

"Klay." She sighs. "I can't. You hurt me bad."

"I know, baby girl, but I'm going to make it right. I swear."

"ATF? You knew?" Scout pulls from my arms and looks between River and Reaper.

River looks down before she looks back up at her

best friend. "I might've kept some things from you. Yeah, I knew."

"We will be talking about this," Scout says, waving her hand between them. She turns to me. "You need to get ahold of Kentucky and find out if he's here, but I wouldn't put it past him. He not only wants to hurt me for defying him but for putting him in prison. He also wants to get even with River for helping me. Vixen would be on his list too. And my Kentucky Chapter President. I'll have to call her."

"Scout, we need to get Skyler, your mother, and you into a safe house." I push toward her and she holds a hand up.

"Clear the room," she orders. River and Reaper stand and start to move out, but Dylan stays back.

"Go," I tell him.

As soon as the door is closed, I'm on her. I take her mouth in a deep kiss, hoping I can get her agreeable if I get her into a sexual fog. She pulls back and I take in her swollen lips.

"Sunshine, I'm not going to let anything happen to you." I don't give her the words that I should because I don't want to scare her off.

"You need to leave. I'm safe here. I have my sisters to protect us."

"We are not done with this."

I move toward the door, pissed that I can't convince her to come with me. As I move out of the office, I see Dylan talking to Frenchie. They met when

Scout got hurt in Palmer. He reaches out to touch her and she steps back.

"Butler," I call his name.

We return to the SUV and pull out. I contemplate how to get her to come home with me or to a safe house.

"You know she's not going to accept you completely until you accept her." Dylan's voice breaks me from my thoughts.

"What?" I turn my eye from the road and toward him before I turn back. We haven't even climbed Hagelberger yet.

"You accept that you both were tricked. You accept your daughter." It's not a question, but I still growl at him.

"Fuck yes, I accept those."

"But do you accept who she is now? She's an extremely talented mechanic and businesswoman. She's been a part of the Handmaidens for years and has never been arrested or even investigated. She's doing things that older women in that club wish they could do."

"I know she hasn't broken the law, that we know of."

"That's not what I said. She's not even thirty and she's the club president. She's managing a brand-new chapter in this wild crazy state." He waves his hand out toward the window. "She did all that plus finished high school, got certifications in mechanics, and raised a very smart nine-year-old."

"How do you know so much about my woman?"

He chuckles. "I pay attention for one, and for two, I looked her up. I did a deep dive."

"I did a background on her."

"Yeah, but you only got what work could give you. I did a bit more."

I slam on the brakes and yank the wheel to the side. "You got your sights set on my woman?"

He laughs harder now. "Fuck, dude, no! You're as bad as that big ATF guy. I have my sights set on someone else, and I had to look up Scout because of it." I pause and wait, knowing he'll tell me. "She saved Minuet. Like not only rescued her from a rapist and murderer but took her in when her family disowned her."

"Shit, I didn't know that."

I get back on the road toward our post.

"How about I watch Ryder tonight and you crash that party?"

I smile at him because he's right. I have to tell her I approve of her life; it's why she thinks I'm the law and she's not. I'm putting the division between us. I don't even address her by her nickname.

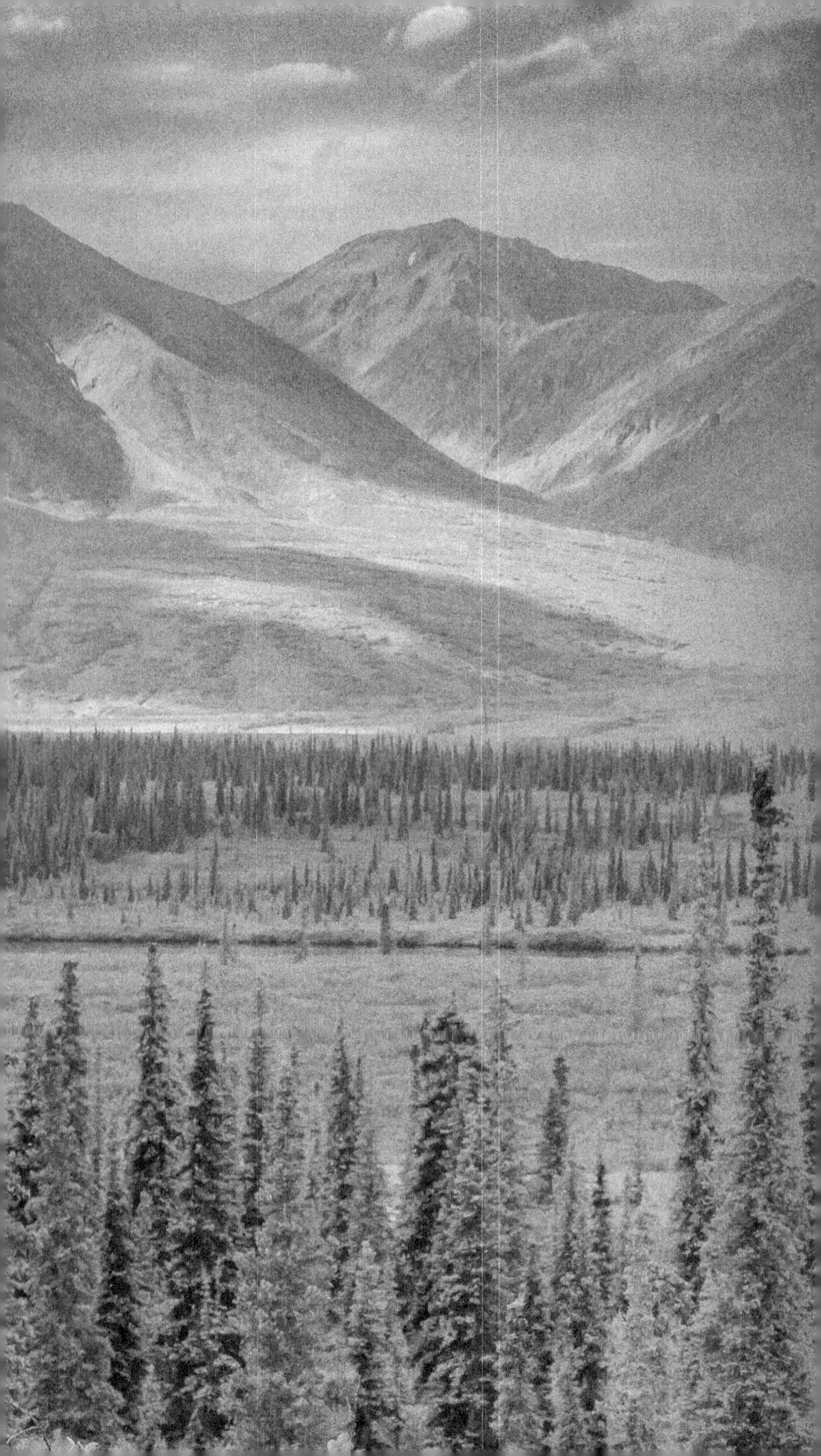

ELEVEN
SCOUT

The music blares around me. Couples are making out, but I stand at the bar, not interested in any of the offers I've received. River and Reaper took off to her room a bit ago. He's going to eat a lot of crow before she lets him back into her bed, so they must be arguing.

Just as I thought, her door opens and they both step out. Her hair is mussed though, so I know they were up to something. There is a lot about them she didn't tell me, and I want to find out. She'll tell me when she's ready. She moves over toward me, while he goes to talk to some guys.

"How are you doing?" I ask her as I slide the bottle of whiskey and a glass toward her.

"I should be asking you that." She laughs as she pours a shot and downs it. I watch her do it one more time before I catch her looking at him. "I can't believe he thinks I'm going to just forget what he did to me."

"What was his reason?" I laugh because I'm kind of in the same boat with Thad. He doesn't understand this part of my life. I can't leave them, but he wants me to. He also wants me to run and hide. I can't and won't do that.

"He was protecting me."

I can't stop the scoff when it comes out, but I stop instantly when I see who walks in the door. I should have been contacted by the gate that he was here.

"Oh yeah, I approved." River laughs and moves off.

I walk right up to him. Taking him in as my high-heeled boots move across the room. He's in a pair of brown Carhart jeans, a long-sleeved blue Henley, and a pair of work boots. His wavy hair is brushed back, and he's not looking at anyone but me. For the first time in a long time, I feel exposed. He has the ability to break me completely, and I know he knows it. But I keep pushing him away.

"What are you doing here?" I hiss low when he's close. He pulls me into his body and smiles down at me. His scent of the pine, outdoors, and him hits me hard.

"I came to hang out with my girl." He laughs like it's no problem he's here.

"You can't be here." I try to move away from him, but his grip on my hips tightens.

"Why not? It's a party meant for everyone associated with the club, right? I'm your boyfriend," he says loud enough that people are watching us. I pull away again and grab his hand, pulling him toward my room. I stop at the bar and look at River.

"Jinx, you got this?"

"We got it," Reaper says from behind her as he wraps an arm around her shoulders. I see a guy who was making a beeline for her turn and walk the other way.

"Come on." I pull Thad down the hall past my office and into my room here at the clubhouse. I push him inside and watch as he takes it in, and I do the same. The room is sparsely decorated with only a dresser, nightstand, and a queen bed in the corner. I stand next to the door, seeing what he sees.

"I wanted to hang out with your friends and get to know them." He sulks and moves back to the door, but I lean against it. I watch his eyes drag up and down my body again. Earlier, when I walked up to him, he took me in and it almost made me flip my hair. Well, if I had longer hair I would have.

"Why don't we stay in here?" I start to push off the door.

"Don't you want me to meet your friends and hang out with them?" His question takes me aback for a moment.

"I do. But you're a trooper, they aren't going to want to relax around you. You are going to have a hard time not thinking about how many laws they are breaking," I state the obvious.

He walks to me and cages me against the door. "I'm only going to be thinking about all the men looking at you in this getup." He drags his hand across my abdomen and under the edge of the tank that barely covers it. "I'm going to think about all the men I'll kill if they see your silky skin," he growls before he leans down, his elbow braced against the door next to my head. Instead of kissing me, he sucks my bottom lip into his mouth and bites it, pulling away slowly. I moan and arch up into him. My hands go to his waist and I hang on to him.

"Since when did you become so jealous?"

"I've always been like this with you, you just didn't notice it before. But I won't share you, Riddler." When he says my road name, I lean up and slide my hands into his hair and pull him down to my lips.

We connect. Our lips brushing each other, over and over. He takes the kiss deeper when he slides his tongue against my lips, and I open for him. I let him lead, giving him everything that I am in this kiss. I want to trust him again. I want him to be a part of my life just as much as he'll be a part of Sky's. We kiss and kiss for longer. Our heads turning. Our tongues sliding. His scruff rubs against my skin, and it turns me on more. His grip on my ass tightens, and I jump up into his arms as he stands to his full height.

I feel him moving and then the bed under me. He helps me from my vest and carefully folds it before putting it over a chair. I'm impressed that he understands the significance of my cut. The way he treats it with the same reverence that I do.

He pushes me back and I fall onto the bed. He lies over the top of me, caging me in. My hands go to his waist and hold on to him as I look up into his blue eyes. Eyes that even though we've been apart for ten years I look into every day because of our daughter. I had no hope of ever getting over him. I saw him in her eyes and in her actions. She's just like him.

"I'm going to hang out with your club. They are going to get to know me. And every man is going to know you are mine. Got it?"

I don't want him to know how much his possessiveness turns me on. I love it. My nipples pebble behind my tank top and my core spasms. But I need to know more.

"Why?"

"I'm not going away. I lost ten years with you and I'm going to try to make up for them every chance I can. So I'll hang out with you here, as long as you don't mind coming with me to AST events? You're my girl again, Scout."

I reach up and press my palm to his scruffy cheek. He leans into it and I see the calm wash over him. "We can't live every day for what we missed. Let's just go from now. We will live our lives every day to the fullest. That's all we can do."

He leans down, pressing into me more, and I love the feeling. "When did you get so smart, Sunshine?"

"That nickname is just yours and only when we aren't around my club. I have to uphold a level of badass and I can't when you call me such a sweet nickname." He chuckles and my body vibrates with need for him.

"It's only ever been yours and only ever will be."

I want to ask him about his ex-wife, but this isn't the time.

"Now I'm going to fuck you hard enough that they do hear you so they know who you belong to," he growls before his lips come to mine. He takes the kiss deeper, demanding my submission, and I give it. In bed I'll always give him what he wants, but outside I'm going to push him because that's in my nature.

I give until we are both breathless and he pulls away.

"Thought you didn't want anyone to hear my sex sounds." I quip back, and the next thing I know I'm flipped over and his hand is cracking against my leather covered ass. I squirm in desire, needing him even more now. He removes my boots and I lie there letting him.

"This time I'll allow it because I need them to know I'll kill them if they try to take what is mine. But don't sass me, Sunshine." He pulls me up and undoes my pants, then pulls them off inside out in one big pull. I fall back to the bed, and he pulls my top off me next. "No fucking bra, Scout?" I look over my shoulder at him and smirk. I watch as he rips at his clothes. His shirt flies across the room, followed by his jeans and boots.

He crawls back onto the bed between my spread legs as I continue to look over my shoulder at him. He lifts my hips and swipes his tongue through my folds. I cry out and fist the blankets. He tongue fucks me a couple of times before he pulls back and slams into me.

I scream long and loud at the intrusion and the fullness. He moves in and out of me in long, demanding thrusts. I can barely hold myself up on my elbows. I fall to my chest and turn my head to the side as he continues his punishing and thorough fucking. I arch my back as he tips my hips and hits a spot deep inside me. I cry out again. He pulls out and I'm flipped around and lifted up. He pushes me down on his cock as he kneels on the bed.

I start working myself on his cock as he uses his hand on my shoulder to pull me down harder on him. I throw my head back and he takes a nipple into his mouth, biting it, laving it, sucking it deep. I can feel my orgasm building. Sweat pours off both of us.

"Please, Thad. Please. I need…" I beg and plead with him.

He pulls me down harder with each of his upward thrusts and my eyes roll. I'm not going to be able to stop it. He's got my body set to live wire and I'm ready blow.

"Come for me, Sunshine," he orders, and I scream as my body trembles and shakes. The colors across my vision blind me for a moment. When I finally feel myself settling, I'm building up again because he dropped my back to the bed and has my knees over his arms as he slams in and out, over and over. Going deeper with each thrust.

Thad

I dig my toes into the bed and tunnel into her body in deep thrusts. My balls are drawing up and I can feel her getting close again.

"Play with your little clit, Sunshine," I growl.

I watch as her little hand goes between us. She strokes her clit a few times until I feel her fingers at her entrance on each side of my cock, squeezing. My eyes roll back and I unload with a growl, sending her over again in a cry of my name. I hated letting anyone hear her, but I want them to know she is mine.

I'll do whatever I need to in order to keep her this time. I drop down, caging her in, before I roll and take her over my body. Her legs lie limp at my sides after I let them go. Her sweaty head rests on my chest that is equally sweaty. I can hear her breathing start to return to normal and our heartbeats sync. She's right, we can't make up for lost time, but we can live every day to its fullest. I'll show her and our children how much I love and need them for the rest of my life. I'll love them to my fullest.

She doesn't know it yet, but I'm never letting her

go. She'll be lucky to make it to Christmas without my ring on her finger. Maybe I'll talk her into having another baby too.

I chuckle against her head at that thought, and she leans up and kisses my chin.

"Let's take a shower." Her voice is husky and it goes straight to my cock. "Maybe I'll get on my knees for you." I'm up and have her in my arms, striding for the bathroom, where she does get on her knees and takes me deep.

I look down at my sleeping Sunshine. I took her so many times during the night, I know she's going to feel me every time she moves today. I couldn't stop myself. It's early, but I have plans for the day. Her beautiful sexy ass is peeking out from under the covers and I smack it to see my handprint.

She comes up crying out and rubbing her ass. Her eyes are shooting daggers at me. And before I know it, she's launching her naked body at me.

"Why are you dressed?" Her sleep-laced voice purrs in my ears.

It's hard for me not to lay her back down and make love to her again. I might have fucked her to begin with, but I insisted on slow and made love to her early this morning. I love both speeds with her. Her body is so receptive to me.

"You need to wake up, Sunshine. We are taking Sunrise and Ryder to the Golden Days parade."

"Sunrise?" she asks, her head cocking to the side. Her short hair is all mussed from my hands and taking a shower.

"Sky is my sunrise. She woke me up to what I was missing in my life. You and her." I kiss her on the neck and suck in the skin slightly.

"Let's just stay in bed for the day."

"Nope. Get some clothes on. We are spending the day with the kids. Dylan will be with us. Do you want to invite your sister, Minuet?"

"The fuck. You kept me up all night. I'm tired and want to stay with you until my mom calls to be rescued from Sky." She huffs as I set her down and she moves to the bathroom.

A short time later she emerges in a pair of jeans and some band T-shirt. She grabs a pair of riding boots with barely any heel and her cut.

"I need to get River to come too, and I have to stop in my office before we go get Skyler." Her short hair is styled and she has on eyeliner and mascara, bringing out her beautiful, light hazel eyes.

"Why do you need to get River?" I watch as she sends a text and moves out of the room. I follow her and hear the snores from several people coming from the big room. She stops at her office and puts her finger to a pad. I hear the click of the lock disengaging. She enters and I follow her inside.

"Why the fuck do we need to get up so fucking

early?" I hear a male voice behind me and turn to see Reaper standing there with River.

"You don't need to come." I turn back and see that Scout is standing in front of a small gun safe. She pulls a gun and slips it into her back where I see the pancake holster.

"You know we are going to a function that will have hundreds of kids?"

"You know I don't go anywhere unarmed. Just like you." She turns back to me, quirking her eyebrow. She knows I always have a piece on me.

"Fine, let's go. Dylan will meet us there with Ryder."

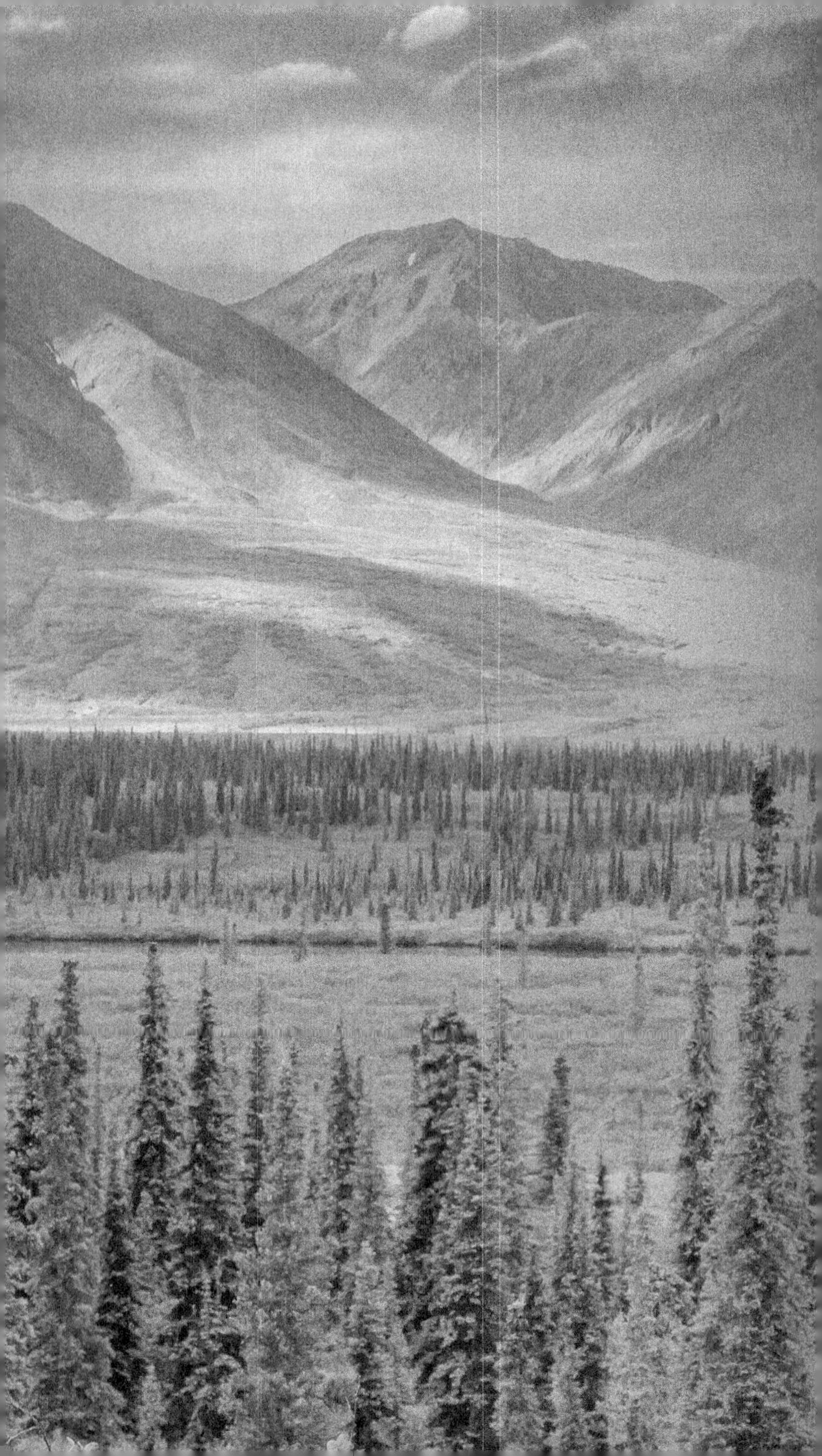

TWELVE
SCOUT

The parade has been a lot of fun. I forgot about the crazy things people do for their floats. When the jailhouse comes by trying to pick up people who don't have a button on, I almost get dragged away because one of the ladies dressed up like saloon girls is a friend of Monica's. I hold my ground and shake my head. She just laughs and moves on. But I catch her watching me when she gets further down Second Avenue. I shake it off and continue to help the kids collect candy and things from people.

Thad has been attentive to Sky and myself, as well as to Ryder. But the real surprise here is Reaper, or Klay. He hikes Ryder up on his shoulders and runs up to several floats to get candy directly from the people. Thad and Dylan join in with Sky. Us girls just sit back and watch laughing.

As the last of the floats goes by us, I don't want the day to end yet.

"Want to take the kids over to the Children's Museum?" Thad asks as if he feels the same way. I nod and the others agree to join us after they grab some more coffee. I watch as Minuet, Klay, and River walk a block further toward the coffee shop. Dylan remains with Thad, the kids, and me.

We are playing for a few minutes in an exhibit when alarms start blaring along with lights flashing. I look around and see that Thad, Dylan, and Ryder are in the next room looking at something. Skyler is climbing on the inside rope gym. I grab her hand as soon as she hits the bottom and we are moving toward the doors with everyone else. People are crowding the front and rear exits when a woman yells out.

"Over here, you can use this side fire exit."

I turn and can't see anything but her back. The door is down a narrow hallway, but I clearly see the emergency exit sign. I move toward the door when I'm grabbed from behind. I struggle, and my body is shifted before I'm flying back. I look to my empty hand and don't see Sky near me.

"Skyler," I scream her name before my body hits a wall and I fall to the floor. Everything hurts. Pain explodes in my head, but I'm up and stumbling for the door. I turn to see a man making his escape from the building. He's tall and dressed in leather. His head is covered with a stocking hat. I slam open the door in time to see Monica shoving Sky into the back of a car. Sky is screaming and yelling. I run for the car, but I'm too late. With tires screeching, Monica races away from the curb. I hear my name being yelled and booted feet coming toward me. My fight kicks in and I swing. Thad takes the hit and wraps around me. I break.

Everything inside me gives up. I scream and cry. "My baby. She took my baby." I don't hear anyone else, but I'm transferred into another set of arms and look into River's sad eyes.

"Sorry, sis," she says, and the crack of her hand against my cheek stops the panic. I'm calm. Deadly calm. Everything slows in my body.

I move to Thad and look up at him.

"Monica just kidnapped my daughter. You better pray you get to her before I do." I turn and look around me, taking in everything as my cell pings in my pocket.

> KEYS
>
> Kid finally got back to me. Motorcycle man had this tattoo on his wrist.

The picture that comes through fills my body with a rage I've never felt before. I hold the phone to River and she starts cussing. Reaper takes it and nods. It's a picture of death with his sickle. The same tattoo that Phantom has on his right wrist.

"I knew he was here."

"What?" Thad asks, and I slip my phone back in my pocket. He'll need to know how we got the confirmation, but I'm not ready to tell him what I really do.

He thinks he knows. He's heard the stories, but he doesn't really know.

"I just got confirmation that Phantom is here. We need to get to the compound and get ready. He'll want me, and I'll gladly give myself up for my daughter.

Thad

I stop talking into the phone and look at her. When her words sink in, I hand the phone to Dylan.

"I got transpo in fifteen. Get help." I grab my girl.

"You are fucking not giving yourself up for *our* daughter." I enunciate the word because Sky is both of ours. "I won't lose my daughter and the woman I love in one swoop." I kiss her hard on the lips and let her go. I need to get to the trooper post, where the helicopter is waiting for me. "You make sure she doesn't do anything stupid. Her life is in your hands until I come back. Take her and Ryder to the compound," I order Reaper, and he nods. The compound is the most fully defensible place we have right now. Reaper knows what I'm currently feeling. I did some searching and I know his and River's little secret.

I'm moving across the pavement, my boots stomping, as Scout yells that she doesn't take orders from me. Dylan slides into the driver's seat and I climb into the passenger seat of his SUV. We head to the post with the lights and sirens blaring.

I call back dispatch and order a BOLO on Monica's car, her, and Stanley "Phantom" Smith. I also request a printout of stolen vehicles to be waiting for me when I arrive. If history repeats itself, he'll be in a stolen vehicle or motorcycle, and I'll find him. He won't get away from me. I read the report on what he did to Scout. He's dead if I get to him. Fuck my badge.

We pull up less than fifteen minutes later and I'm running for the helicopter. I'll take the controls, while Dylan has a fixed wing plane waiting for him at the small airplane strip.

I jump into the helo and see the reports. I quickly scan them before lifting off. I start a grid search pattern over the city. I hate how time-consuming this is going to be. I want to call Reaper and make sure he has Scout safe, but I focus on finding my daughter.

A thought hits me and I go with it. I hand my phone to my copilot and instruct him to dial Monica's cell and triangulate her location when she picks up.

The call goes to voicemail and I have him try again. I'll blow up her phone until she picks up.

"Thad, if you promise to marry me, I'll give her back." Monica's voice sounds tinny over the speakerphone, and I'm thinking she's in an area with little cell service.

"I want my daughter back, Monica. You don't want to do this."

"He told me if I get her, he'll take care of everything," she whines, and I look over the area. Still nothing.

"He's a murderer, don't trust him.

"Gotta go. He just pulled up. I'll tell him we made a deal and—"

A gunshot rings out and I hear screaming.

"Skyler," I yell.

"This isn't how the game is played." A deep voice comes across the line before it goes dead. My copilot dials back, but it immediately goes to voicemail.

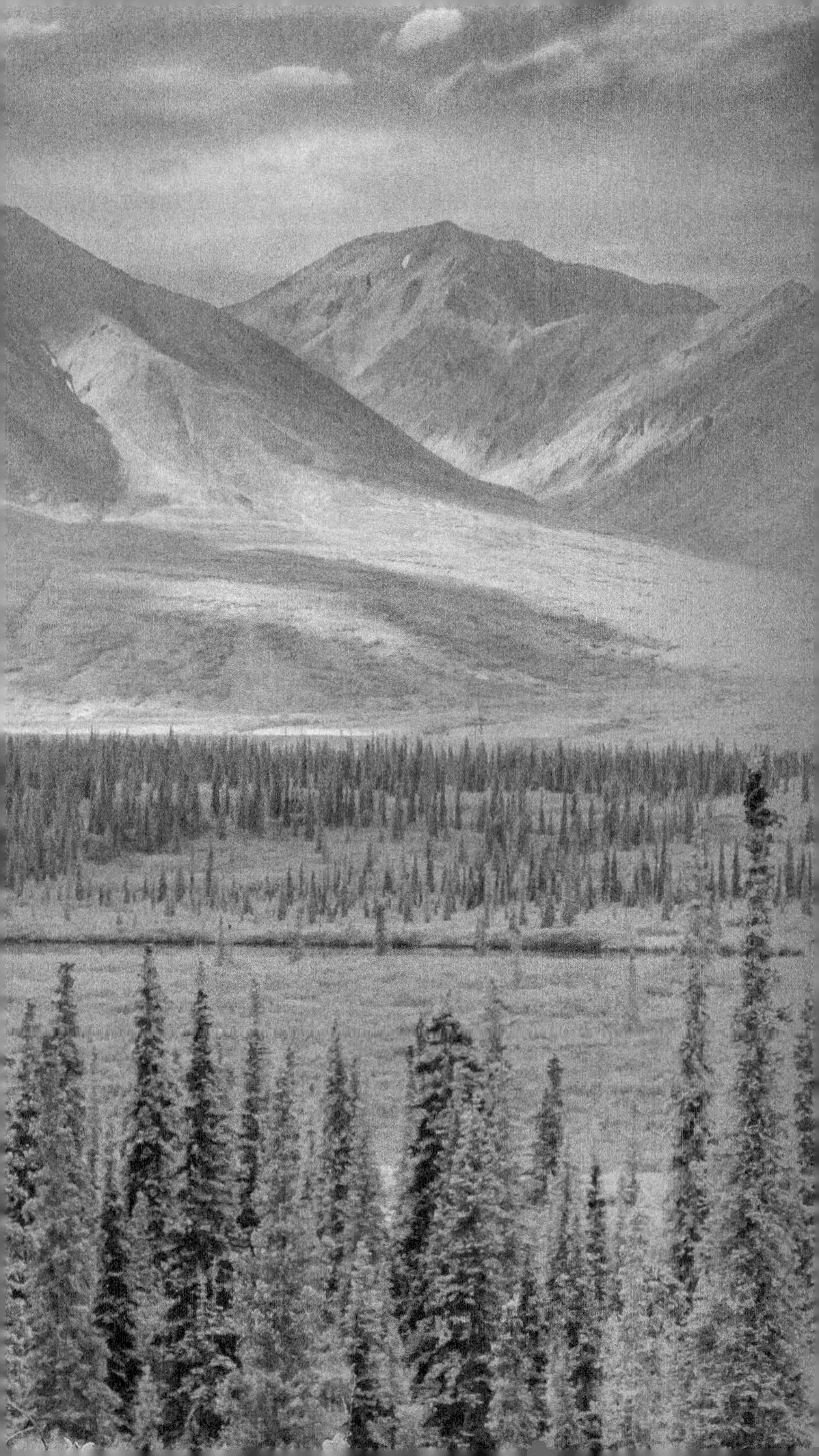

THIRTEEN
SCOUT

Thad is barely out of the parking lot when I'm dialing Keys.

"I want a location on the fucker working with Phantom," I bark the order and move toward the bikes. I'm holding tightly to Ryder. I can't and won't lose him too.

"On it, Prez. He's been hiding from the authorities, but I pinged his IP earlier. I think I know where he's hiding." I hear the clicking of keys across the line and look at everyone around me.

"Frenchie, take Ryder and go to the compound. Guard him and my mother in my place. I want Keys, Poison, and Badger backing you up. Make sure Scarlett arms them up. Lock it down. You know how. No one in or out but a Handmaiden."

She nods and moves toward Thad's truck.

"Please bring my sissy and daddy home," Ryder says as he hugs me.

My heart clenches. This little guy is stuck in my heart too. I hope I make it through this to watch him grow, but I highly doubt it. If I kill Phantom and Monica, I'll be going to jail for a long time. But if it saves my family, I'll do it in a heartbeat.

"Okay, got it. What else?" Keys says as a ping comes across mine and River's phones.

"Jinx and I are going to get the fucker to tell us where Phantom is hiding. Reaper is with us. I want Vixen, Rivet, Scarlett, and Ginger on standby in Fox. I expect he'll call me and want to do a trade. I'll need my bike, some chaps, and lots of weapons. You heard I want you there directing us all."

"On it." She hangs up, and I look at the two people standing with me.

"Sorry, Jinx, I'm on your bike and you're riding bitch with one of us. We are heading toward Badger Road."

"Get on, baby." Reaper points at his Harley V-Rod with Ape hangers and an extra-long seat for a passenger. Jinx's bike doesn't have a bitch seat, so she'll be more comfortable on his.

"You promise me you'll keep her safe." I hear her ask him, and he whispers something to her before she climbs on the back of his bike. She's wearing a helmet he pulled out of his saddle bag for her. I grab hers and put it on.

We take off, and less than ten minutes later we are pulling down the side road alongside a small convenience store that's been here since before I was born.

We pass several houses before we come to a trailer sitting on a small plot of land. I park and pull my gun before I walk to the door and kick it in. I don't give a flying fuck about neighbors calling the police or anything. I've got a one-track mind.

Get my daughter back.

The idiot screams like a girl from his computer setup, and I grab him. Reaper stomps in behind me and I swear the shitass almost pisses himself.

"I want to know where Phantom is hanging out. Where is he having you take the girls?"

"I can't," he whines. "He'll kill me." He shakes in my hand, and I press my gun under his chin. I stare him in the eyes.

"He just kidnapped my nine-year-old daughter. I'll kill you if you don't tell me. If you do, at least you'll live."

"You'll take care of him?"

"Yes." I have no doubt in my mind. I'm not afraid of the decisions I'll make.

"Fine."

He tells us. But just in case he tries to double-cross us, I drag him from the trailer with us.

"Reaper, Jinx, follow along." I push him through the driver's side into the passenger of his little Cobalt and then climb into the driver's seat.

I'm about to take off when my cell rings. I look down and see an unknown number on the screen. I text Keys as I accept the call. I pull away and head toward Fox, where I can get my bike. The plan worked out better than I could've known. When this idiot told me where Phantom was hiding, I almost smiled, but I didn't want to give anything away.

"Yeah." I have my gun pressed against the idiot's head to keep him quiet. This could be Thad checking up on me, but I'm fairly certain I know who it is.

"Hello, my beautiful little Scout." Phantom's voice comes across the line. I hear crying in the background and my spine straightens.

"She better be crying because she broke a nail, or I'll shove my gun against your balls and shoot."

"Now, now, my little girl. You know not to talk to Daddy that way." He acts as if the years apart were of us missing each other and not what they really were. I hated the fact that he insisted I call him Daddy. I'm not opposed to that kink, but with him there was no way. He was sick and tortured me.

"You aren't my daddy. You killed him."

"See, you need a replacement."

"Where are you?"

"Ask me nicely, little girl." His voice holds a bite to it, and I want to choke on the vomit rising up my throat.

"Daddy, can I come see you?" I add an extra sugary sweetness to my voice. It's hard to concentrate on driving and talking to him.

"Meet me at the Chatanika dredge. One hour. Alone, or she'll no longer be crying. On your bike so you can't hide anyone in that truck of yours. No cell. No communication. I have a signal blocker. Follow the surveyors tape." That last part I knew because the idiot told us he procured it for Phantom.

"Yes, Daddy," I say the words I know he wants to hear, but I hate that everyone is listening into our conversation and will know.

He hangs up and I do too before my cell is ringing again.

"We are waiting," Vixen says and hangs up. I follow behind Reaper and Jinx on their bikes as we make the thirty-minute drive to the Fox weigh station. It's closed, so it's the perfect place for us to meet up.

We pull up and I jump out, dragging the guy with me.

"Cuffs." I hold out my hand and a pair of zip ties land in my palm. I cuff his hands and feet, then push him into his back seat.

"Call the troopers to come get him after we leave," I say into my earpiece.

"Got it," Keys says.

I take a deep breath and focus on getting my chaps on next. My black bike is waiting for me. I hate that I might have to bring Sky out on the back of it, but it's the only choice I have.

"I'm heading out," Reaper says after he kisses Jinx hard. The plan is for him to get as close as he can then hike in. I'll then come in next. I notice he's now got a five-gallon bucket strapped to the back of his bike where River was seated before.

Hopefully, because of the beautiful weather and all the other bikes on the roads, Phantom won't question the sound of a random bike in the valley. There isn't a lot of cover. The trees are bare bean poles out there, but this was the best option we had.

I continue to gear up. I slip the shoulder rig on with my dad's gun in it, then I put on my leather jacket and cut. I hear the blades of a helicopter approaching and wonder if it's Thad.

I don't have to wonder long when my cell starts ringing.

"What the fuck are you doing?" he says in way of greeting.

"Doing what I need to. I love you too." I hang up on him and slam my phone against the pavement. It's a little dramatic, but I want him to see what I'm doing so he won't try to call again.

River's phone goes off, and she answers it.

"I know. He called her. They have a meeting. You can't go, or he'll kill Little Bear." She walks away and I look at Vixen. I need to go, or I won't make it on time.

"Take care of my mom and Little Bear. Keep an eye on him too." I nod toward the sky.

"I'll see you again." Vixen kisses my cheek, and I give a two-finger kiss wave to the helicopter before I mount up and head out.

The road twists and turns, leading me deeper into

the wilds of Alaska. I see several moose off in the brush. The nearly thirty-minute drive takes less even though I'm trying to coast and act like I'm not in a hurry, which I am. The helicopter only followed along for a couple of miles. Part of me wishes he were here. That I could kiss him one more time, but I can't focus on that. I need to concentrate on our daughter and Phantom.

I pull up to the Chatanika Lodge and look across the street to where the dredge is back off the road. I leave the bike. The shot rock trail isn't very good on a bike.

The hike has me crossing private property, but I'm not afraid of anyone. Honestly, I'm not afraid of Phantom. I'm afraid for my daughter. It's a good half-mile walk and I'm heavily armed with two guns and two knives, in full riding leather, and not dressed for this. I make it to the dredge and see Monica's car along with a motorcycle. A body lying on the ground has me running. It's Monica. Her face has been blown away. I hold a hand over my mouth and see a trail that I follow. This is the only place he could be.

As I move further away from the road and into the thicker pucker brush, the more I'm glad that Reaper is somewhere close by. Or at least I hope he is. I've been hiking for another fifteen minutes. I'm a good way from the road now and can barely hear the vehicles in the distance. There are pockets of areas around me without trees from the dredging process. The trail of surveyors tape has me moving away from the dredge and following a small creek.

I finally hear crying in the distance, and I can't stop my legs from pumping harder. I know better than to run into a blind situation, but I pass through the trees and there she is tied to one, my baby girl. I look around but don't see him. I know I'm not thinking straight as I run for her and drop to my knees.

"Baby, Momma is here. I got you." I hold her face in my hands and only see dirt on her, no marks, but I'm still worried.

"He killed that woman," she cries against me. I'm about to stand when two things happen at once.

A gun presses against the back of my head and Sky screams. I lift my hands slowly out to my sides and lean away from my daughter. This is where I either fight for our lives or trust Reaper.

"Step back, little girl," Phantom orders as he too takes a step back. I know the gun is still pointed at me. And this close, he'd kill us both.

"I'm right here, Sky, baby. Just wait, it'll be okay."

She nods at me as her tears flow and she sobs.

"Don't hurt her. You promised," I say as I step away from her and lace my fingers behind my head. I shift so that if he shoots me, the bullet won't hit Sky too.

"You cut your hair. Bad girl." He slams the gun into the side of my head, and for a moment I see double and fall to my side. Sky is crying harder, but I try to block her out as I focus on channeling the pain. I focus on meditative breaths so I won't lose consciousness, and I stand back up. With this hit and the one from the museum, I'm going to be sore later.

I turn around and take him in.

"You grew out your hair and beard." I point out to him. His normally trim hair goes to his shoulders and hangs down in a stringy mess. His beard looks more like mange.

He cocks the gun and points it at Sky. I jump in front of her. I know the shot will kill us both. But if it hits me first, at least I could slow the bullet down as it goes through my body.

"No." I shake my head, ready to beg. "You killed my father."

"I killed more than him. Killed a young girl. Broke her jaw, just like I did yours. She wouldn't shut up. I left her body for the critters north of Ptarmigan Falls, off one of those domes. Killed the man who owns the cabin about a mile from here. Left him in his fucking shitter." He points to the north. I try not to think about how serious this is right now. I focus on getting my daughter out of this situation.

"Let Skyler go. Take me to the cabin, show me who my daddy is." I try to distract him with sex.

I step toward him, but he fires the gun in the air. He walks up and pistol whips me with the side of the gun. I fall to the ground and slowly stand up again. I'm not going to let him see what he's done to me. He's closer to me, and I fake that I'm going to fall forward. He leans over and I come up fast. The back of my head slams into his face. I watch the gun fall through my blurry vision and I work on pushing him away from it. I need to hold him off until Reaper reaches us. Hopefully, that gunshot gave him an idea of where we are.

Phantom swings on me, hitting me in the kidney. I cry out and twist with a punch aimed for an uppercut. The bastard steps back and my fist grazes his nose. I follow up immediately with my other hand aimed for his throat. He isn't prepared and falls back choking. It's a stunning blow but doesn't drop him. He rushes me, and we fall to the ground grappling for control. He grabs my hair and laughs in my face as he rises up.

"I'm going to fuck you in front of your little girl before I kill her."

I aim and my fist nails him hard in the crotch as he's standing over me. He cries out and crumples to the dirt. I rush for Sky as he nurses his crotch. I reach under my jacket and pull my knife to cut her loose. She points over my shoulder and I turn, blindly throwing the knife as a gunshot rings out.

I look down expecting to see a hole in my body, but I see nothing. I look at Sky and there is nothing on her either. I look back to see Phantom fall to the ground again. Reaper moves out of the brush carrying the bucket.

"We only have a short time. Your man will be pulling up to the lodge in about ten minutes." He sets the bucket down and drags Phantom's body to the very tree Skyler was tied to. My knife protrudes from his shoulder. Reaper's bullet hit him in the back. But he's starting to come around.

Reaper ties him to the tree and I just watch, wondering what he's doing. "Grab the bucket. I saw a grizzly moving this way. Little Bear, go stand over there and don't look," he orders my little girl. She moves toward the trail I came up.

I lift the heavy bucket. I can barely carry it and end up dragging it to Reaper. When he lifts the lid, I see the old grease from the kitchen and know what he has planned. Reaper pulls my knife from Phantom's shoulder and wipes it on the ground. Together we dump the grease over Phantom's head. He sputters and yells at us about how we won't get away with this.

Reaper punches him in the face and Phantom's head falls to the side. If the troopers make it here in time, they can get Phantom to a hospital and he might survive. But then he'll live to come after my family again, and I can't let that happen. I don't care if I'll have his blood on my hands.

We walk off until we get to the creek, where Reaper cleans the bucket thoroughly and leaves it without any of our prints on it.

"This way, it's quicker." Reaper points at a trail, and we make our way out.

When we reach the road, we walk on the shoulder. Hopefully, someone is waiting for us. I'm not really sure I can take Sky on my bike with me in the condition I am. I don't regret what we did and I never will.

Thad

I can't believe she didn't listen to me, but then again, I can. The woman is going to be the death of me if she survives this. I slam the SUV into park and jump out next to her motorcycle in the Chatanika Lodge parking lot. I look around and toward the dredge. I'm rushing across the street when a voice stops me.

"Daddy." I turn and look up the road. Walking along the shoulder is Scout and Reaper, who is carrying my daughter. I run for them and grab Scout in my arms. Reaper hands me Skyler and I hold them both.

Scout is covered in blood and barely holding it together. Sky is covered in dirt but looks okay.

"We have a body." The message comes across my radio, and I'm worried I'm going to be parted from Scout because of the law I'm tasked to uphold. "Female. Gunshot to the face." I look at Scout.

"It's Monica. He killed her," she says softly.

"Where is he?"

A bloodcurdling scream rips through the valley.

Scout and Reaper look the other way as I face the direction the scream is coming from. Scout starts dragging me toward her bike.

"He's dead," she says.

"How? What happened?" I ask her, reaching for her arm to stop her.

"He beat up Momma. Reaper saved us," Skyler says in her sweet voice. "He killed that bad lady who took me, and he said he killed other people," she continues, and I worry about the nightmares she's going to have.

An ambulance pulls up and the crew starts treating Scout.

The radio on my hip squawks again as I hear motorcycle pipes approaching in the distance. "We have a fresh bear kill, but we can't get the grizzly to leave it."

"That'd be Phantom," Scout says.

"We should take her in," the EMT states.

"Nope. I need to take my bike back. If you want, I'll go in after that." She climbs out of the back of the ambulance, not caring that she's moving slow. That she won't be able to hold up her bike very well, and she's still recovering from several broken ribs from several weeks ago.

The motorcycles pull in and her truck is bringing up the rear. Rivet moves toward Scout's bike. "Nope, Prez, take your expensive ride back to Fairbanks. We got your bike."

River is looking around, her eyes wild, and she advances on Scout. "Where is he?" she demands.

Reaper took off to get his bike as the paramedics treated Scout. He said he'd be back in a bit. We all turn when we hear the pipes of another motorcycle approach. Reaper is barely stopped and River is jumping in his arms, kissing his face. He holds her tight to his body as they talk quietly.

I want to kiss and hold my girl, but she needs to be evaluated more before I can do that. Once I get my hands on her though, it will be a while before I let her go again. I will blister her butt for what she did, but then I'm going to make love to her.

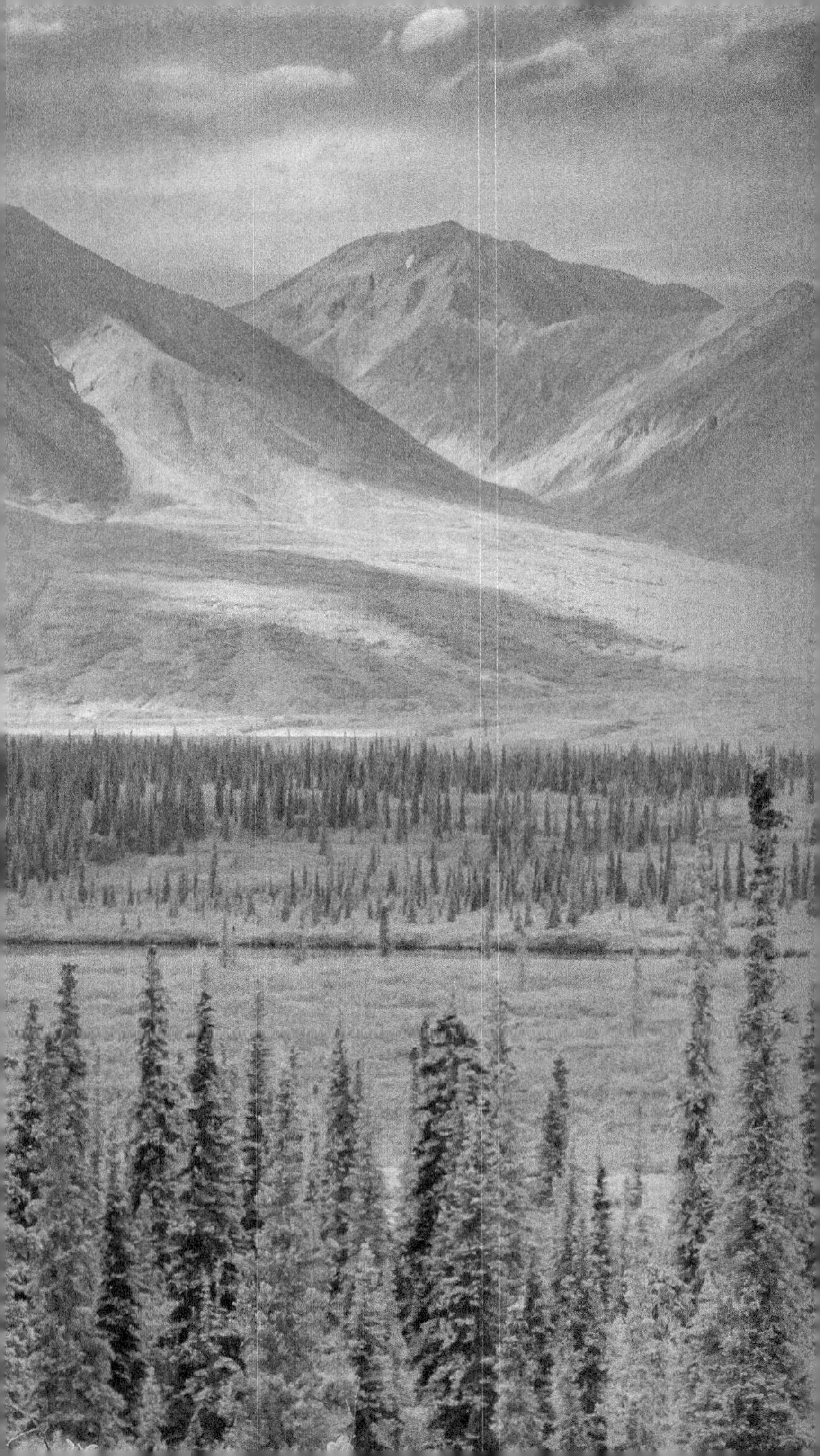

FOURTEEN
THAD

Hours later I'm holding her against my body in her bed. She doesn't have any broken bones but is one giant bruise with a concussion. I thanked Reaper for saving my girls, and he just shook his head.

"Have a feeling you are a part of my family now, lawman." He laughed. It's funny that he's calling me lawman when he was law until just recently.

When we got back here to the compound and her home above the garage, she insisted on lying in her bed with the kids in her arms. Skyler doesn't have any physical injuries, but we both know she watched him kill Monica and was terrified watching him attack Scout. Come Monday I'll be finding someone for her to talk to because I don't want her to suffer. Ryder clung to both of them and it made me realize how much he needs a mother in his life. Scout has only been around him a few times and he's already looking at her for that comfort. She's not afraid to give him the love that he needs. The three of them laid in that bed with myself or Violet lying with them off and on until the kids fell asleep. I carried Skyler to her room and then Ryder to an open bedroom Violet said he could sleep in.

Now I'm lying here thinking of everything that happened. They found parts of Phantom's body. His kill was determined to be an accident. According to Reaper and Scout, he had a bucket of kitchen grease and was going to use it to get rid of Skyler. Scout said when she was fighting with him, they knocked the bucket over and he ended up in the grease. He was braced up against the tree when they fled from him. He never expected Reaper to show up and help or for Scout to fight back as vehemently as she did. There are troopers still out searching for the old miner's body and for the young girl we are pretty sure is Avery's sister. Phantom was on a killing spree and was going to kill anyone blocking his path to Scout and his revenge for her putting him in prison.

"No," Scout cries out and jolts, her body trembling.

I wrap her in my arms and she clings to me, wrapping around me like a blanket. I'm worried she's going to struggle with the fact that she didn't intend to kill Phantom and yet he died because of his own actions.

"I'm here, Sunshine." I kiss the top of her head and she settles down.

"I was scared." Her voice trembles and I look down to see her looking up at me. Her eyes shining in the late-night brightness. "But I wasn't scared to die or kill him." Her words give me pause. "I was scared for Skyler and of never being right here again. I don't want to live without you again. I can't. I won't survive it."

I lean down and kiss her, a soft kiss that she takes deeper. She rolls me to my back and straddles me. She pulls her shirt over her head, leaving her in tiny sleep shorts and a thong. I help her out of those, being careful of her injuries, and then slide my sweats down and watch as she impales herself on my cock. We make love slowly. Her riding my cock. I watch as her body tightens and every emotion crosses her face, but I see the love most. After she comes, I hold her hips and move up into her a couple more times before my balls pull up and I explode inside her. Marking her as mine from the inside out.

"I love you, Thad." I hear her soft, sleepy voice.

"I love you too, Sunshine." I kiss the top of her head before I pull the blankets up over us, and we fall asleep with me still buried in her and her lying on me.

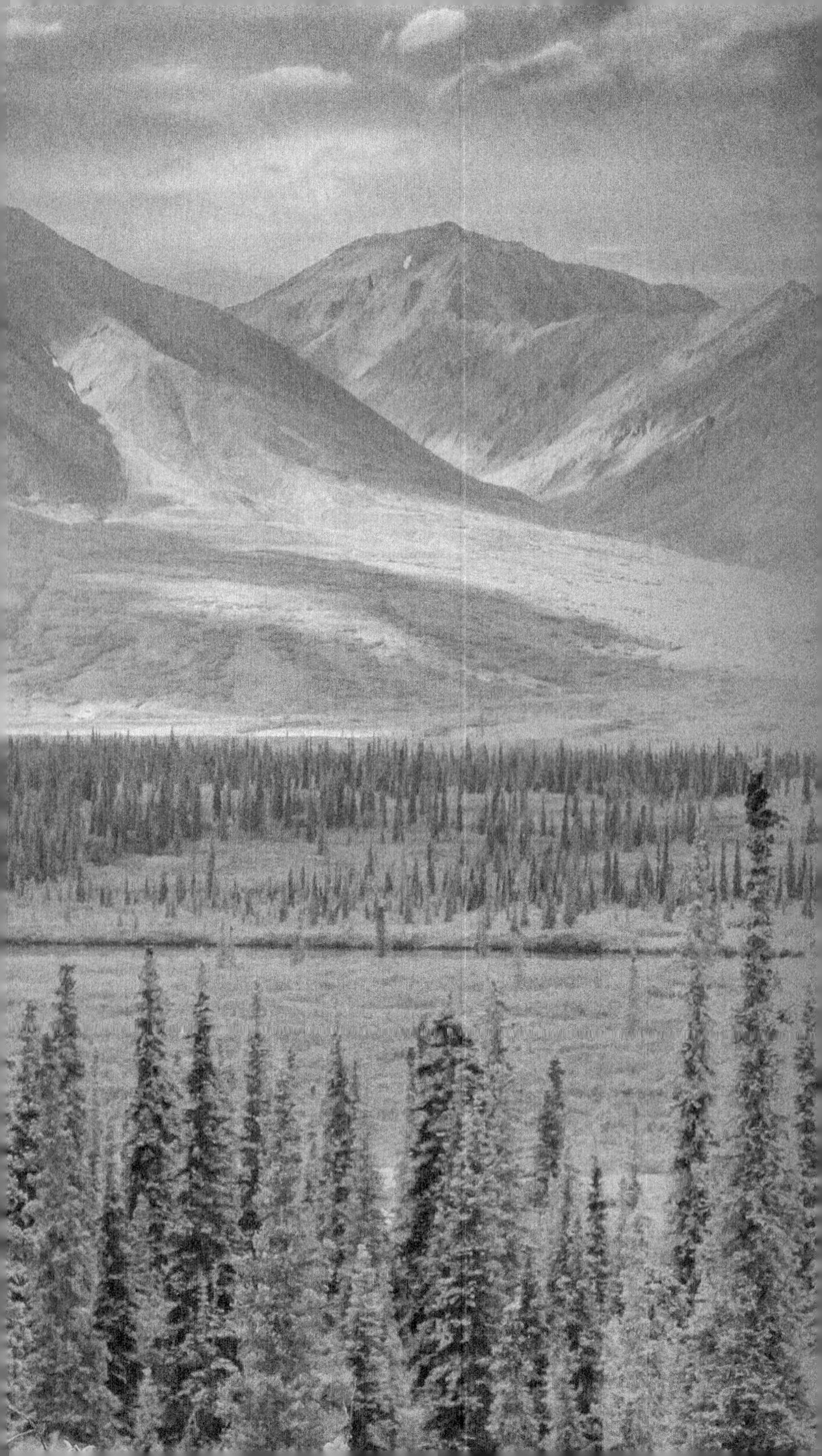

EPILOGUE
SCOUT

5 MONTHS LATER

The Christmas lights shine on most of the downtown businesses as I move out of the clinic. I look down at the engagement ring on my finger. Thad didn't wait even a month before he was proposing and moving into my place. His dad is living at his place while he goes through his divorce, and their family home is up for sale. My mother is still living with us. But come spring, we will be breaking ground on building her a house on the property so she doesn't have far to travel to the café.

I look down at the paperwork and images in my hand. I knew my shot was due months ago, but Thad and I were still discussing if I wanted another baby. We have one of each. Sure Ryder isn't physically my son, but we are already looking into me adopting him. I love him like he's mine.

"Scout." I hear my name yelled, and I look around as I shove the paperwork into my bag. Running toward me is Avery. She has taken the road name Badger very well. She fought to have as much of her sister's remains returned to her and held a funeral for her. "I got it." She jumps toward me and I brace myself. We are about the same height, but she's on the skinnier side.

I hug her and smile because I know she had an appointment with a potential investor. I tried to give her the money, but she insisted she do it herself. I look over her shoulder and smile at my uncle's partner. She did all the business portfolio paperwork and cost analysis for the tattoo parlor. So coming soon to Ptarmigan Falls will be its first tattoo parlor. I'm going to be happy with that because it means I won't have a damn pain in my rear hanging out in my garage as he stares down River every day. Reaper does tattoos and will be working with Avery.

"Congratulations." I smile at her and move toward my truck. I pull myself up into it and look around. There was a time I thought I'd never be back here and another time when I thought I didn't need to be here, but this is my home. It will always be that and now I get to raise my kids here. I peek into my purse and the image of my new peanut looks back at me.

I need to go get my baby daddy the correct way this time. I'm not taking no for an answer because he knew what he was doing every time he didn't put on that damn condom, just like I knew too. And this time only he will get the information first, no one else.

I decided to ambush him at work and handed him the pictures folded up. I've never seen him happier, and he insists we get married as soon as possible. I can't deny him. He's always been the love of my life.

This time it will work out and we are going to raise our children together. I might have been wrecked before, but the collision didn't kill me and I've learned to trust and love again.

I really appreciate you reading Wrecked. Please don't forget to leave a review. To continue reading more from Devil's Handmaidens MC Alaska Chapter, grab the next book in the series here, Rattled. For a complete list of my books, along with series lists and reading orders on my website.

You might want to consider signing up for Surprises from E.M. for a free story as well as first chance at cover reveals, releases, contests and more.

ACKNOWLEDGMENTS

Thank you so much to Erin Osborne and Martha Lanham for setting up with collection and letting me join. I loved exploring the world of MC and writing a story that takes place in my beautiful home.

Next, I want to acknowledge my husband and kids. Shaun, Paige, Kelsey and Dani have been a huge support and put up with the crazy deadlines I set for myself. I can't thank each of you enough for your help with this one. I finally got to put the bear scene in a book.

My editor Nadine has been with me since the beginning, six years now you've dealt with my lack of commas or overuse. Thank you for the excessive number of scripts I've been dropping on you the last couple of years. We are finally getting there. People know us. Thank you!

Someday way way way in the future my granddaughters might sit down and read this, and I want them to know that I thought of them. Every tough girl

I write is for you. I want you to know that you can do anything you want. Anything!

To the couple of men, I call sons, thank you so much for putting up with my endless questions about torture, guns, knives, motorcycles, and everything else you help me with. If it wasn't for you, I wouldn't have thought of the grease. Thank you, Koda, James, Cory, and Cody.

To my extended family (mother, brothers, fosters, nieces, nephews, cousins, aunts, uncles, those that aren't but should be, those that I call by other names and finally those I count as) all of them everywhere thank you for your kind words, support, and not blocking me.

To Krystal thank you for being my best friend. For putting up with my endless calls and questions. I don't know where I would be if you hadn't congratulated me six years ago. You've become a part of my family and I love yours. I can't wait to hug you soon.

The Rally Pack and A-Team, you all are awesome, and I really appreciate all you do for me. Thank you for posting and ARC reading. Someday we'll meet in the real and I'll hug you if I haven't already. I say this all the time, but I mean it so much. You are amazing.

Author and PA friends who help me with promo

and questions thank you for all your support. I love our community.

To you the reader, thank you for taking the time to read Wrecked. I hope Riddler and my first MC met your expectations. Don't forget to check out my other books for more bada$$ tough girls. If you're not a Baddie come sign up for my Facebook group. https://bit.ly/EMBaddies or my newsletter Surprises https://bit.ly/SurprisesfromEM.

Finally, to that being out there some call him by name, and some don't. I call him my guide and my light. Thank you for this talent and this opportunity.

ABOUT E.M.

E.M. Shue is an Alaskan award-winning romance author. She is proudly featured in K Bromberg's Everyday Heroes World, Aurora Rose Reynolds' Happily Ever Alpha World, KL Donn's Mafia Made Series, Susan Stoker's Special Forces Operation Alpha World, and the soon to be released Devil's Handmaidens MC Collection.

She published her first book in 2017 after having a dream that later became the Beverley Award winning, Sniper's Kiss. Since then, she has gone on to win this award three more times with different books and has published over thirty titles.

Join Surprises from E.M. to be kept up to date on all her new releases and appearances.

https://bit.ly/SurprisesfromEM

ALSO BY E.M. SHUE

Securities International Series

Sniper's Kiss: Book 1

Angel's Kiss: Book 2

Tougher Embrace: Book 2.5

Love's First Kiss: Book 3

Secret's Kiss: Book 4

Second Chance's Kiss: Book 5

Sniper's Kiss Goodnight: Book 5.5

Identity's Kiss: Book 6

Hope's Kiss: Book 7

Forever's Embrace: Book 7.5

Justice's Kiss: Book 8

Duchess's Kiss: Book 9

Kiss of Submission: Book 9.5

Truth's Kiss: Book 10

Kiss of Secret's Past: Book 10.5 (Coming July 2024)

Knights of Purgatory Syndicate

A Seductive Beauty

A Tortured Temptress

Santa Claus, Indiana Stories

Coal for Kiera: Christmas of Love Collaboration

Hanna's Valentine: A Santa Claus, Indiana Story

Hailey's Rodeo: A Santa Claus, Indiana Story

Love in a Small Town

Caine & Graco Saga

Accidentally Noah

Zeke's Choice

Lost in Linc

Completely Marco

Jackson Revealed

Trusting Jericho

Mafia Made

Her Empire: Mafia Made 2

His Rebel: Mafia Made 5

Her Exile: Mafia Made 8

Tattoos & Sin Series

Doctor Trouble

Vegas Jackpot

Doctor Sinful

Frozen Heart (Coming March 2024)

Stand-alones and Anthologies

Until Tucker: Happily Ever Alpha World

Until Lydia: Happily Ever Alpha World

Rocco's Atonement

Distracting David

Taliah's Warrant Officer

Forever Finn's Kisses

Discovering Tyler

Artfully Bred

Beyond The Temptation: Volume 2 (Blinded by Secrets)

Devil's Handmaidens - Alaska

Off Balance

Wrecked

Rattled

Ruined (Coming November 2024)

Ramsey University Series

Virtuous

Tenacious (Coming April 2024)

Ambitious (Coming May 2024)

Russian Cardroom Series

Ante

Drawing Dead

All In (Coming June 2024)

Prominence Point Rescue Series

Confined Space

Grid Search (Coming September 2024)

Shiver of Chaos

Gambit's Property (Coming August 2024)

Printed in Great Britain
by Amazon